The two most important days
in your life are the day you are born
and the day you find out why.
—Mark Twain

Vernazza, Italy

THE
VERNAZZA EFFECT

A Novel

ROBERTA R. CARR

To Andy, my partner in all things

ONE

I silence my morning alarm, glancing across the bed with fingers crossed. *Oh, good. He isn't moving. I caught a break.* One foot is on the floor as a hand grips my arm. "Not so fast."

Not fast enough.

My husband wrestles away my pajamas, doing nothing—no foreplay, no tenderness—to prepare me for sex. He enters my body, which he calls his pleasure palace. His breathing grows jagged and irregular until he convulses into a loud orgasm, making me feel like roadkill once again.

Will hovers over my face, acting as if he's about to kiss me. Instead, he dips lower and bites my nipple.

"Ouch!" I shove him away. "That hurt!"

"At least I know you're alive." He rolls over to his side of the bed and closes his eyes.

I want to smother him. What makes him think it's okay to treat me this way? Why do I put up with it?

A hot shower washes away my frustration. I eat my usual bagel breakfast, make a salad for lunch, then walk to my car. It's chilly with overcast skies as I ease onto Highway 101 for my morning commute. After passing through the rainbow tunnel, San Francisco's famous bridge and skyline emerge, a stunning view that takes my breath away. I glance at my wedding ring, sighing. Will used to affect me that way.

We first met when he stopped for lunch at the café where I worked during college. He wouldn't leave until I agreed to a date. We went on a romantic picnic at the top of Mount Tam, followed by ski trips to Tahoe, concerts, and candlelight dinners. I fell in love and married my Prince Charming.

Over the past four or five months, his overnight business trips have increased and he talks less about them. He comes home late without explaining why. Instead of making new memories on our days off, he prefers to stay home and watch sports on TV. Is he bored after only six years of marriage? How do we get back on track?

A few sailboats have ventured onto the bay, slicing through small whitecaps. Cars, cyclists, and pedestrians share the Golden Gate Bridge. Luckily, the sky has cleared so visitors see the iconic views. There have been days when everything—including the bridge—was hidden behind a mayonnaise-dense fog for hours.

I pass through a toll booth, drive several miles, and turn right on Divisadero to begin the steep, uphill climb to my hospital. I nab a coveted spot in the parking garage and take the elevator to the NICU where I've worked as a neonatal nurse for five years. Two colleagues grumble about starting another shift as we change into scrubs. Not me. This place is my haven.

I'm walking to my usual post when my supervisor, Anne, approaches me. "Morning, Ella. A micro-preemie was admitted last night. I'm assigning you."

"But... What about Sophia? Yesterday, she had a high temp. I'd like to stay with her until she's stable."

"She'll be fine. This new one needs your expertise more." Anne gestures across the unit. "He's waiting."

Sophia has been with me since birth; I've grown close to her and the family. Although I want to ignore Anne's order, I get how things work. The new baby's health must be dire for her to reassign me.

From the moment I see the little guy, I understand why Anne pulled me. He weighs only one pound and eleven ounces—less than Sophia's birth weight. He looks like an old man with his paper-thin, wrinkled skin. Wired stickers cover his chest, arms, hands, legs, and feet to monitor his vital signs. I'll be feeding him through an umbilical line until he is weaned from the ventilator. He's a fragile one, hanging on by a thread.

In the early afternoon, I hear a commotion on the other side of the unit. Various machines blare; panicked voices fill the air. The dreaded 'Code Blue, NICU! Code Blue!' sounds over the loudspeaker. My breath halts. Which baby is in trouble?

Staff is running here and there, shouting. A doctor and two nurses surround an incubator. *Oh, no! It's Sophia!* A third nurse arrives with a respiratory therapist, pulling a crash cart. The doctor shouts CPR orders. I want to help but can't leave my baby or we'll have two codes. I'm fraught with worry as Sophia's life hangs in the balance.

Then the unthinkable happens. The response team steps away from the incubator; the doctor shakes her head, talking about septic shock. A nurse glances at a wall clock and writes in a chart. I choke back tears. He's recording Sophia's time of death: June 12 at 2:08 p.m. Her body is wheeled away, a precious life ending before it ever really began.

I struggle through the rest of my shift, then drive home with a broken heart. First, Will's behavior this morning, and now Sophia's death. It's too much to bear. I swerve off the highway toward my sanctuary, the Marin Headlands.

A cool breeze blows as I sit on a bench and stare at the bridge. To the right is my hospital. Across the water is a silhouette of East Bay, my hometown. On my left is Mill Valley where I live with Will. This panorama usually centers me. Not today.

Would Sophia be alive had I been with her? Maybe, maybe not. I'll never know for sure. I wipe away a tear, barely able to accept she's gone. Losing a patient is the hardest part of the job; it's something you never get used to.

A half-hour later, I'm still on the bench. I can't face Will. Not until I get my act together. I call my best friend.

"Hey, girl!" Tara answers with her usual zeal.

"Any chance for an early dinner?"

"Ella, what's wrong? I know something's up."

"Not over the phone. Dinner?"

"Where and when?"

"How about The Spinnaker? Five-thirty?"

"See you soon."

As the owner of a family law firm with twelve attorneys and support staff, Tara is always busy. I count my blessings when she makes time for me. Will resents me hanging out with friends—especially Tara. This evening I want to talk with someone who listens and that's not my husband. I text him about dinner, hoping he doesn't push back.

I take in the view for a few more minutes. Losing Sophia saddens me, yet it's more than her death that weighs me down. My heart aches for a loving partner and a chance to raise a family. Is that too much to ask? Life isn't meant to be easy but does it have to be this hard?

TWO

The Spinnaker restaurant is located in Sausalito, a picturesque enclave on the water. I get us a table with bay views and order Pinot Grigio, our favorite wine.

Tara arrives wearing her lawyer uniform: a tailored black suit with a white collared blouse. Her long, curly hair doesn't match her professional demeanor. She catches my wave and hurries over, sitting across from me.

"What's hubby done now?"

I pour wine into her glass. "Will isn't why I called. It's work. One of my babies died this afternoon."

"Oh, Ella. I'm so sorry."

Tara Collins and I have shared a lot during our twenty-five-year friendship. My home was her haven when her eight-member clan overwhelmed her. I joined her family parties after the loneliness of being an only child kicked in. We've always had each other's back.

"You treat those babies like your own." Tara twists a ring on her finger. "Maybe it's time to start a family."

A server approaches the table, bringing sourdough bread. "Good evening, ladies. I see you have wine. There's fresh salmon if you're interested."

I nod, not caring what I eat.

"Sounds great for both of us," Tara says. "We also want privacy, okay?"

"You got it."

Tara dips bread in olive oil. "Ella, let's get back to kids. Why not begin the adoption process?"

"Nothing's changed. Will won't budge. He's worried about getting a drug baby. Or a child with bad genes."

"He's stalling. Agencies conduct a rigorous screening process. You need to push back."

I briefly close my eyes. We've had this conversation so many times and it never goes anywhere. She gets to make unilateral decisions because she's single. "I don't want to discuss Will."

"Easier said than done when I watch him control your every move."

The salmon arrives, giving me a respite from her interrogation. Once the server is out of earshot, Tara continues. "Admit it. Everything's about him, what he wants."

I rub my temple to soothe the tension. I shouldn't have called her. She is wound up from work, acting as a lawyer instead of a friend. "Please. Can we talk about something else?"

Tara drains her wine glass. "How's your mom?"

I push away my half-eaten meal. "Not good. She's on around-the-clock pain meds."

Tara finishes her dinner and sets her plate aside. "Ella, I'm worried. You have a controlling husband, your mom's dying, and the one place that gives you solace—your job—is taking a toll. This isn't okay. Everyone has a breaking point."

Mine just arrived. I pick up the check to pay on the way out.

"C'mon, Ella." Tara follows close behind. "I only want the best for you!"

Even though she means well, I don't want another lecture. I get plenty of those at home. I stop in front of her MINI Cooper. "I appreciate you meeting me for dinner."

She throws her arms around me and doesn't let go. "Losing Sophia sucks. You pour so much love into those babies. I wish I could take away your pain."

I cling to her, tears blurring my vision. "You just did."

She drives away; I sit in my car to watch a pretty sunset. Does heaven exist? Is Sophia surrounded by angels and unicorns? I hope so. When the last bit of orange drifts from the sky, I start the engine. Tara would go ballistic if she knew how Will treated me this morning.

THREE

Ours is such a cute house, three bedrooms, two baths, tucked into a wooded hillside with hidden paths. Mom gave us the down payment as a wedding gift. A football game on TV broadcasts to an empty room.

"Will, I'm home."

He saunters barefoot into the living room dressed in jeans and a tight black T-shirt. "How's the obnoxious one?"

I hang up my sweater feeling like Will and Tara's tennis ball as they compete in the Ella Open. "Something happened at work. I needed to talk."

He swigs beer. "What's the crisis this time?"

"Remember Sophia? The baby that was born at twenty-four weeks?"

"No, but do tell."

"She's been with me since birth. Last night a new baby was admitted. Anne assigned him to me even though Sophia had a high fever. I know why she did it but I didn't think she would—"

"Ella! I don't have all night!"

I sit on the couch. "Sophia died today."

"That's it? That's the reason I ate leftovers?" He settles into his leather recliner with a beer. "Classic Darwinism, babe. Survival of the fittest." He focuses on his 55-inch HDTV instead of me.

Even for Will, this is a new low. I slip away to the bathroom, fill the tub with steamy water and lavender foam, and ease into my oasis. I pop bubbles, pretending they're my problems. If only the real ones disappeared so easily.

My cotton pajamas warm my skin as I walk to the kitchen to take a vitamin with some milk. Sleep is my second-best friend these days and I know her well.

Will shouts from the living room, "Hey Ella. Come watch the game's end. It's a nail-biter."

"Not tonight. I'm exhausted."

He gives me a once-over. "You might as well go to bed alone wearing those crap pajamas."

I'm not taking the bait.

I'm asleep when Will bounces on the bed. "Wake up, wifey. You owe me. This morning I had sex with a corpse. You can do better." He wears a sneer and nothing else. "Big Willy missed you."

"I told you I had a—"

"Shh. No talk. Give your hubby some luv." He pushes his crotch into my face, forcing me to pleasure him.

"Ahh... So good... Just what I needed." He rolls on his back. "Give me a sec for round two."

Pretending another round won't happen is a pipe dream. Usually, I cooperate to get it over. Tonight, the wild look in his eyes frightens me. "Will, please don't—"

"I said no talking." He yanks my pajama top hard enough to pop its buttons, then kicks off the bottom. He spreads my legs extra-wide, pinning my hands above my head.

I close my eyes as he has his way with me. There's no other way to describe his version of sex. He gets off on dominating me, pushing limits without leaving marks. He's making up rules and changing them daily. I better do something—maybe get counseling—before his behavior escalates.

My phone rings in the middle of the night. "Yes, hello? Who is it?"

"Ella, it's Mae. Margaret has taken a turn for the worse. You may want to come over."

My sixty-two-year-old mother has end-stage pancreatic cancer. I knew this day was coming, yet Mae's call shakes me to the core. "I'll be there soon."

"Who in the hell was that?" Will turns on a bedside light, squinting.

"Mae thinks we're losing Mom." I roll back the covers. "I have to go."

He rubs my shoulder. "Babe, I'm sorry. I'll get dressed and drive you."

FOUR

Mom's porch light is a bright star guiding us to her house. The neighborhood is eerily quiet as we hurry inside. Her pale, skeletal body brings me to tears. Three days ago, she was sitting up and talking. Now she's barely conscious. How did she wither so fast?

"Sorry for calling in the middle of the night," Mae says. "As you can see, she's gone downhill fast."

"No apologies. You've been a wonderful caretaker."

I pull a chair next to the bed. "Hi, Mom. I'm here."

She opens her eyes and smiles, whispering inaudible words, then drifts to sleep.

"It's the morphine," Mae explains. "If I don't give it to her, she's in pain."

Mom's labored breathing tells me she's near the end. Months ago, she had come to terms with her impending death. I thought I had, too. Now, I'm not sure. She is my compass.

I pull out my phone and scroll to the playlist she and I created. Mom loves the classics, and she adores Martin Lass' new-age violin music. I begin with her favorite Lass piece, "Sonnet." The melody has a calming effect on us.

At daybreak, Will drives home to get ready for work. I call my supervisor to request time off. I'm not leaving Mom's side.

Two days later, my mother takes her final breath. The moment is surreal, my anguish indescribable. I lay my ear against her chest, hoping for one last heartbeat. There's no sound, no movement, no hope. Just like baby Sophia, Mom is gone, plucked too soon from the earth.

"I'll notify the funeral home," Mae says. "Do you want me to call anyone else?"

"Would you mind texting Will and Tara?"

I stare numbly at my beloved mother, unable to accept she has passed yet I'm so grateful we had this time together. We emptied our hearts, leaving nothing unsaid. I find solace knowing she is no longer suffering.

Will rushes into the room an hour later. "Hey, babe. Got here as fast as possible." He gazes at mom's body. "What can I do?"

"We need to call Chapel of the Chimes to schedule a service."

"On it." He pulls out his phone. "Anything else?"

"No, only that."

When the mortuary staff arrives, I kiss Mom's cheek one last time, the hollowness in my chest expanding every second. A torrent of fresh tears arrives as a new reality sets in. The one person who loved me unconditionally, the one person who offered wisdom and security, the only person who never judged me is dead. I'm a twenty-nine-year-old orphan.

FIVE

On June 19th, mourners gather to say a final farewell to my mother who will be buried alongside my father. She wanted two classical pieces played at her service: Barber's "Adagio for Strings Op. 11" and "Clair de Lune" by Debussy.

Mom loved roses. Two of her favorites, *Double Delight* and *Mr. Lincoln* are placed on her casket, filling the air with a sweet fragrance. Tara releases doves to symbolize Mom's departing soul as well as the easing of my sorrow. She wasted the sentiment on me.

Following the service, guests gather at a reception. I force a smile, half-listening to stories about my mother. There's an outpouring of kindness, yet I've never felt so alone. That orphan sensation returns with a vengeance.

Will is a gracious host, chatting with guests and answering questions. Although he and Tara have been civil to each other, their tension is palpable, both vying for my attention as guests start leaving. It's time to separate them.

I huddle with Tara in a corner. "I couldn't have gotten through this day without you."

"Want to stay at your mom's house tonight? Drink wine and reminisce?"

I shake my head. "I'm going home. I'll call soon."

She wiggles her phone. "I'm available. Day or night."

I give her a long, appreciative hug before sending her on her way.

Will and I meet with the mortuary staff to wrap things up. Their job is finished, handled with efficiency and dignity, papers signed, the dead buried. Now, it's up to me to keep on living.

As Will drives home, I stare out the window, watching the world pass me by. Mom's death has left a gaping hole in my heart that no one can fill. Why didn't I spend more time with her? Now, it's too late. She's gone and is never coming back.

"You're quiet, babe. Everything okay?" His voice is calm, comforting.

"I miss her so much, Will."

"Yeah, you two were close." He clasps my hand.

He's been my rock during this tragedy; I couldn't ask for a more supportive husband. Who knows? Mom's death might be the catalyst that brings us closer, her final gift to me.

SIX

I have a fitful night, dreaming about doves, somber music, and caskets. My chest tightens as I imagine life without my mom.

"Mornin', babe. You're up early." Will folds me in his arms. Soon, Big Willy is awake, too. "See what you do to me?"

He's a gentle lover, moving in a sensual rhythm reminiscent of our early years. I'm ready to whisper this in his ear when he finishes quickly and pushes up on an elbow.

"So, wife, how do we settle Margaret's estate?"

Huh? The abrupt shift from sex to business throws me off balance. "I suppose I should meet with her attorney."

He tugs my ear. "It's good to have a second pair of these listening to that legal jargon. I bet if you called, he'd see us today."

I swing my legs over the side of the bed. *Why is he pressuring me? I buried her yesterday. He doesn't—*

Will snaps his fingers in my face. "Earth to Ella."

"Mom just died, Will. I'm having a hard time concentrating."

He kisses my neck. "Don't worry. I'll keep you focused."

At three o'clock, Will and I walk into the office of Edward Abrams, Attorney at Law. Although I don't know him well, he has handled my family's legal matters for as long as I can remember.

"Good afternoon, Ella. Your tribute to Margaret at the service was quite moving."

"Thanks, Mister Abrams. This is my husband, Will."

"Yes, we met at the reception."

Will clasps my hand. "I'm here to support Ella. We have questions about her inheritance. We also want to know if we can sell the Piedmont property. Right, babe?"

What? I shake his hand free. *Where's that coming from?*

"Let's take this one step at a time." Mr. Abrams sorts papers on his desk. "Ella, did you and your mom discuss the estate?"

"Not really."

"Okay. Let me explain some things. Your parents created a Revocable Living Trust that transfers assets to you upon their death. Have you read it?"

"No. I've never seen it."

"Here's a copy. Margaret created a second trust called an Irrevocable Charitable Trust. She did this for a couple of reasons. First, to save money on taxes. Second, and more importantly, she did it for you."

"For me? How?"

He passes over a second document. "Your bout with cancer deeply upset your mother, Ella. She's been donating money to the American Cancer Society on your behalf for years."

Hearing this news stirs painful memories of why I'm unable to have children. It also reveals my mother's generous spirit. "I had no idea she did that."

"She'd hoped to see a cure in her lifetime. It's such a cruel turn of events for her to die from—"

"Can we move this along?" Will interrupts. "Get to the bottom line?"

I shoot him a look. The lawyer seems as shocked as me by his insensitivity. I motion for Mr. Abrams to continue.

"Ella, your mother's estate is valued at six and a half million dollars."

Will twitches like a runner in starting blocks. "Uh, did I hear right? Six and a half *million*?"

Mr. Abrams hands me a spreadsheet, ignoring Will. "You inherit five million, which includes the Piedmont property and a financial portfolio. The American Cancer Society gets the rest."

Will flies to his feet. "There's no way we're giving away a million and a half bucks. How do we reverse that?"

"You can't," Mr. Abrams explains. "This is how Margaret wants her assets distributed."

Will links his fingers behind his neck, blowing air through his mouth. "What about the house? Can we sell it?"

"Ella inherits the property to manage as she chooses. There are several legal steps we must take such as determining the date-of-death value—"

I hold up a hand to halt the conversation. Too much is happening at once. "Sorry to interrupt. May I have a couple of days to read the trusts? To let this news sink in?"

The office grows quiet enough to hear bubbles from the salt-water aquarium.

Mr. Abrams looks at me, at Will, then sits back, rocking. "That's an excellent idea, Ella. Take whatever time you need."

Will cracks the knuckles in both hands, his veins straining against his neck. Although he's ready to explode, I'm not letting him pressure me. There's too much at stake. I shake Mr. Abram's hand. "Thanks for seeing us on such short notice. I'll be in touch soon."

Will storms out without saying a word. He gets into his BMW and slams a fist against the steering wheel. "Can you believe Margaret? Giving away money when she has us?"

"We must honor her wishes, Will."

"Bullshit. I say we hire a lawyer to prove she was demented. I mean who gives away that kind of cash?" He glares at me. "And what's with that 'let everything sink in' crap? Why didn't you let Abrams finish?"

"Please, let's go home. I'm tired."

"When aren't you tired?" Will shoves the car in reverse, burning rubber as we exit the parking lot. He zooms in and out of traffic, exceeding the speed limit.

"Dammit, Ella, why can't you deal with this shit? What's your problem?"

Breathe. Don't set him off. "You're right. Taking care of business is important." *On my timeframe, not yours.*

"Glad you know it. And don't ever embarrass me in front of Abrams again!"

"How'd I embarrass you?"

"Don't play coy. You know what you did."

"No, I don't. Please explain."

"Focus on getting the house in your name so we can sell it. I want the money."

My hand flies to my mouth. My mother's grave is warm and all he cares about is her estate? I'm free-falling off a cliff and no one is here to catch me.

"I'll delay my business trip to get this moving." Will passes over his phone. "Call Abrams. Get on his calendar for tomorrow."

His words breed panic. I want him gone so I can think without him pressuring me. "You said the Oregon trip is important, that your boss wants a signed contract. You should go. I'll read the trusts while you're away."

He downshifts, taking a corner too fast.

"It's three days, Will. We'll meet with the attorney when you get back."

He races through a yellow light. "Fine. But I expect action. I mean it, Ella. Don't push me on this."

SEVEN

I get up early the next morning and drive Will to SFO. He refuses to park his pricey convertible at the airport, fearing someone will scratch or dent it. Why not hire a driver instead of expecting me to chauffeur him? He has an expense account. His babbling—*Drive faster! Pass that idiot! Did you pack my blue suit? Don't call or text, I'll be too busy*—grates on my nerves. Where's an ejection button when you need it?

As he disappears into the terminal, I breathe a sigh of relief. Having three days without him badgering me feels like sunshine after a rainy week. I tossed and turned last night, worrying about so many things: life without Mom, what to do with her house, why she didn't show me the trusts. On top of that, I'm scheduled to work on Monday. How am I supposed to take care of preemies if I'm not sleeping or eating?

I try making sense of everything on the drive home but my mind jumps all over the place like a swarm of hungry grasshoppers. I choke back tears as I approach UCSF. Mom and I toured the campus when I expressed an interest in their nursing program. We spent an entire day observing classes, meeting professors, and eating in the cafeteria. She wanted to do a "reality check" to make sure the six-block university was a good fit for me. I'll never pass by my alma mater without thinking of her.

The school is quiet today because of summer break. Normally, students pour into the streets causing traffic to—

That's it! That's the answer! Why didn't I think of it sooner? A break from work is exactly what I need. Time to pull myself together, to silence the monkey mind. Will won't like me taking an unpaid leave, but this decision isn't about him or money. It's about my ability to function. For now, those babies are better off without me. I set a course for the hospital.

My supervisor isn't in her office, which doesn't surprise me. She's a busy lady. She arrives several minutes later. "Sorry for keeping you waiting, Ella."

"No problem. I appreciate you making time for me. And thanks for attending my mother's memorial. It meant a lot."

"It was a lovely service." Anne sits behind her desk. "Your text sounded urgent. What can I do for you?"

Breathe. Trust your instincts. "My mother's death hit me hard. I'm feeling overwhelmed, not sleeping. Plus, I have to settle her estate. I'd like to take a leave of absence."

"How much time are we talking about?"

I take an extra breath. "Six weeks."

Anne flinches, glancing at a stack of papers.

My leg bounces like a spooked kangaroo. I plucked that number from thin air, maternity leave for new moms. *Is three weeks enough time for me to function? To not cry at the drop of a hat? What if—*

"Go to HR and complete the paperwork," Anne says. "You wouldn't ask unless it was important."

"Really? I'm willing—"

"You've been through a lot, Ella. Losing a patient and a parent in the same week would traumatize any of us. If you need emotional support, Employee Assistance provides counseling."

I leave Anne's office and walk straight to HR to complete the paperwork. How many times did Mom say to take better care of myself? She'd be proud of me for stepping back. Distracted nurses make mistakes. I won't do anything to jeopardize my babies' welfare.

Mom also encouraged self-sufficiency. Why didn't she mention the trusts before she died? What was her intent behind the Charitable one? She left the house to me instead of donating it. Does that mean she wants me to keep it? Would selling the property upset her? Luckily, I know a wise woman who will shed light on this topic. I set a course for Tara's office with an offer I hope she can't refuse.

Oakland is a culturally diverse town with well-tended parks, ancient redwoods, Lake Merritt (a large, tidal lagoon), and million-dollar homes. It's also the tenth most dangerous city in the nation with a crime rate nearly four times the national average.

Tara's law building is located smack-dab in the middle of town, part of a mixed-use redevelopment area. Her queendom is certainly a busy place with phones ringing, voices drifting from offices, and people scurrying around.

I stick my head in Tara's office. "Surprise!"

"Ella! Nice surprise indeed!" She comes around for a hug. "What brings you to the shady part of town?" She sits on the edge of her desk and motions to a chair.

"I dropped Will off at the airport and want to drink wine and reminisce with you. Care to join me for a slumber party tonight?"

Her smile fades. "Bad timing. I'm preparing for court tomorrow. Big case. How long will the evil one be away?"

"Three nights."

She studies her calendar. "What about the day after tomorrow? I wish I had—"

"I'll take it!"

"Where's Will vacationing this time?"

Talking with her about my husband seldom ends well. It's time to switch topics. "I met with Mom's attorney. I need help deciphering the language you lawyers use to confuse the rest of us mortals."

"You want to talk *without* hubby around?" She raises an eyebrow.

"Let's just say he and I are moving at different speeds."

"Music to my ears." Tara wiggles her foot, glancing at her watch.

"You're busy so I'll get going. By the way, I took a six-week leave from work."

Tara gives me a thumbs-up, not questioning my decision whatsoever. She's behind her desk typing the second I step out of her office.

Our professional lives are so different. Most days I clock in, do my job, and go home, putting the workday behind me. Tara's world is a non-stop conveyor belt of daunting responsibilities. Not only does she manage a heavy client load, but she shapes the practice with her vision, community involvement, and work ethic. Her ability to juggle everything amazes me.

I should go home and tidy up, but I'm drawn to Mom's house. I have clothing and a toothbrush there. What else do I need?

I pass familiar streets, stores, and homes that dot Piedmont's hilly landscape. Attending schools that overlook the bay, struggling through piano lessons, getting braces, and growing up with my best friend is part of my life in this tight-knit community.

An overwhelming sadness hits as I park in Mom's driveway. She isn't in the house waiting for me with homemade soup or oatmeal cookies or a warm teapot. No sitting at the table, catching up on our lives.

The next-door neighbor steps on her front porch with her French bulldog and waves. "Hello, Ella. Margaret's service sure was special. Ollie and I are keeping an eye on her house for you."

I pet the dog. "Thanks, Susan."

"Will you be selling?"

"Don't know. It's too soon."

"If you decide to list it, a gal in our bunco group is a realtor. I'd appreciate you keeping her in mind. We ladies support one another and that includes you. If you need help, don't hesitate to ask."

Everyone wants to help, and there's nothing anyone can do. I must face these ghosts on my own.

EIGHT

An immovable silence greets me as I walk inside the house. I open windows to let in the fresh air then move from room to room, observing things that usually go unnoticed.

Mom enjoyed living on this quiet, tree-lined street with friendly neighbors. The pale-yellow kitchen, white cabinets, and hardwood floors made her happy. She liked having a formal dining room even though she rarely used it. My room hasn't changed since I moved out.

Mom's bedroom looks nothing like the makeshift hospital Mae had cobbled together five months earlier. The commode, walker, and wheelchair are gone. The folding table with medical supplies has disappeared; the hospital bed returned. I pull a sweater from a drawer, pressing Mom's scent to my nose. How will I survive without her?

A social worker told me the parent-child bond is the most fundamental social tie. She said losing a parent is like losing a part of yourself, that I might experience confusion, fear, depression, relief, or anger.

An odd detachment from ordinary living floats through me. I've always had peace of mind knowing Mom was a phone call away. Those days are gone. I lie on her bed, hug her sweater, and close my eyes. Will wants to sell this home. Do I?

When I wake, it's dark outside. I flip on lights and close windows, stopping to microwave a frozen lasagna for dinner. Afterward, I return to Mom's bedroom. A chest in the corner catches my eye. I wonder what's inside?

A cedar scent wafts out as I open the lid. The space is tightly packed, yet organized. My school report cards and class pictures crowd a baby book and knitted blanket next to a cheerleading outfit and a candy striper uniform. There are keepsakes from my dad: a jacket, a wedding ring, pictures, letters he wrote to Mom. I drag my finger across his handwriting, missing him.

What's this? I pull out a stack of journals. Oh my gosh. Mom recorded life events for years. What a treasure trove! I pick up the first one, settle in a chair, and begin reading.

> *Today starts a new chapter of my life. Instead of staying on the farm, I moved to the city and enrolled in nursing school to follow my dream. Where will this journey take me?*

Mom writes about her classes, fellow students, doctors, and patients. She says nothing about dating or having fun. Instead, she pursues her studies with a laser focus. I had no idea she was so career-driven.

After graduation, she became a surgical nurse at the hospital where she did her clinical hours. Two years later, she quit her job, strapped on a backpack, and flew to Europe. By herself!

She visited England, Amsterdam, France, Germany, and Italy. She gushes about Italy—the food, the art, the good-looking men—more than any other country. She singles out a town called San Gimignano, saying it was special. She had mentioned this trip over the years but I paid scant attention. I'd give anything to hear her stories now.

After returning from Europe, she worked at a teen wilderness camp where she met my father.

> *From the moment we laid eyes on each other, I knew he was "the one." His parents died in a car accident when he was sixteen but that didn't stop him from pursuing his goals. He has integrity, a strong work ethic, and a BIG heart. He is handsome as they come, without an ego. He's husband material and I'm snagging him.*

Her word choice gives me a chuckle. Who says 'snag' to describe a boyfriend? They fell madly in love and were married at city hall four months later. Talk about a whirlwind romance!

Mom was the main breadwinner while Dad finished college. She brags about his finance degree from UC Berkeley, calling him her 'brilliant capitalist.' He bought an insurance franchise six years later, proving her right.

Wow, I had no idea she had two miscarriages. She quit her job when I was born, calling me her miracle baby. She dotingly recorded my sleep habits, feeding schedule, first steps, and other milestones. She traced my hand until my twelfth birthday, after which time I refused to cooperate. Even though I stand by that decision, I admit watching my hand grow is fun.

Mom became a school nurse when I entered third grade. Strangely, I never thought of her as a working mom, probably because we had similar schedules. Her notes about our summer vacations in Kansas bring back fond memories. I can almost feel the warmth of my grandfather's hand as we walked to the barn to milk his cows. He'd leave a bowl of white gold (his term for milk) for the feral cats, and carry the rest in metal buckets to the cellar where a machine separated the liquid into skimmed milk and cream.

Mom wrote about birthdays and anniversaries as well as everyday moments such as strolling on Piedmont's pink sidewalks, cooking with dad, and planting gardens. She stopped writing for a year after he died, saying it was too painful to record life without him. I don't recall her ever crying. We soldiered on during that bleak period, establishing new routines. She probably saved her tears for a pillow.

Mom got creative in later years, taping photos beside her entries. She profiles my pets (a cocker spaniel named Ginger, two cats, a guinea pig, and a blue parakeet). Other photos include school projects, dances and proms, Tara elected class president; me her campaign manager. Mom recorded such great memories.

She also posted painful ones, chronicling my ovarian cancer—the diagnosis, chemotherapy, hysterectomy—in excruciating detail.

> *Knowing Ella will never carry a child breaks my heart. I wish she'd attend a support group to boost her confidence. If she talked with other cancer survivors, she might not feel so isolated. I've tried to guide her but I'm running out of ideas. She vacillates on everything—food, activities, her future. She's talking about dropping out of college for a year. On her father's grave, I won't let that happen. I'll drive her to class every day if necessary.*

Mom goes on and on, making me sound like a nut case. Who wouldn't be depressed after what I went through?

Oh, boy. She didn't like Will, not even in the beginning. She rambles about him, turning her frustration into pages of caustic words.

> *Ella's boyfriend reminds me of a balloon: colorful on the outside and filled with hot air. She's in her room crying because he was a no-show again. He'll strut over here tomorrow as if he owns the place, bringing flimsy excuses and cheap chocolates. He'll take her on a fancy date and she'll forgive him as usual. Why does she pander to him? Can't she see he is a charmer without substance? I wish she'd find someone like her father.*

It's five o'clock in the morning as I read Mom's last entry.

Yesterday my daughter married a man who will break her heart. William Walker is a self-serving narcissist who thinks the world owes him. He doesn't have a compassionate bone in his body. I still can't believe he didn't invite his mother and brother to the wedding. Mark my words, he'll disrespect my girl the same way, dragging her down to his level.

But Ella is a grown woman who has made her decision. I must accept this marriage so I don't alienate her. What I won't do is record the inevitable drama that will follow. It's time to end these musings. Signing off forever, Margaret.

Mom's final words punch me in the gut. She warned me about Will's erratic behavior countless times. Why didn't I listen? Is this why she chose not to discuss finances or the trusts with us? She'd turn over in her grave if she knew how he behaved in the lawyer's office. Or worse, how he treats me behind closed doors.

Unable to sleep, I put on a coat and go for a walk, ending up at Crocker Park in front of Beniamino Bufano's whimsical bear-family sculpture. Mom's journals captured the essence of our family. Envisioning her as a young woman puts her life in perspective, helping me to cope with her death. At the same time, I feel as if I've been flattened by a steam roller. Do I have low self-esteem? Am I afraid to confront issues?

I return home with an urge to keep busy. I explore the contents of each room, then putter in the backyard, trimming roses and pulling weeds. I climb into the treehouse Dad built. When did the space shrink?

In the garage, I admire the framed puzzles hanging on the walls: The Grand Canyon, Keukenhof Gardens, Neuschwanstein Castle, Taj

Mahal, Eiffel Tower, and other world-famous sites. Barbie treasures—dolls, wardrobe, sports car, dream house—are boxed in the attic. Mom kept my last bike, a Cruiser with a wicker basket. Many memories are stored inside this dusty garage.

I walk to the kitchen, pour a glass of iced tea, and make my way to the backyard swing. I'm exhausted from lack of sleep, yet revived by my discoveries. My parents gave me a wonderful childhood. They were great role models, encouraging and loving. Living with them in this neighborhood has given me every advantage.

Will's childhood was the opposite. His father abandoned the family, leaving his mom to fend for two boys. Living in a trailer, watching men come and go, and dealing with his mom's alcoholism traumatized him. He has worked hard to build a better life. I understand why he wants to distance himself from her.

I can't ignore Mom's journals, though. She didn't exaggerate about Will's manipulative behavior. And, if I'm honest, I choose the path of least resistance if he and I disagree because (this is hard to admit) I'm frightened of him. That's no way to live. When we married, he said he wanted a partner; it's time I acted like one.

Even though my parents are gone, their spirits live on inside of me. I can honor their memories—and be a better wife—by standing up for myself, beginning with this house. I'm not ready to let it go.

NINE

Waking up in my childhood room makes me feel sixteen again. I thought life was hard with homework, rules, and curfews. Ha! I never had it so easy. I throw on comfortable clothes and stroll to the kitchen. A hard-working lawyer will arrive in an hour; I can't disappoint her.

At nine-fifteen, the front door swings open. Tara steps inside wearing jeans and a Mills College sweatshirt.

"How'd the big case go?" I slide an overnight bag from her shoulder.

"Knocked it out of the park." She studies me with those wily green eyes. "When you texted about staying here, I worried I might find you in the fetal position."

"Not me. I had a breakthrough yesterday."

"How so?"

"I found old journals mom kept. I learned a lot about her—and me. You should see what she wrote about us."

"Secret journals. So mysterious!"

"We'll look at them later. Let's eat before the food gets cold."

We fill up on banana muffins, scrambled eggs, bacon, and strawberry smoothies while taking a trip down memory lane.

"Remember the first time we baked your mom a birthday cake?" Tara says. "We were what? Eight? Nine? We made such a mess in this kitchen!"

"Don't forget about the lemonade stand. We squeezed so many lemons our hands hurt."

"Didn't you buy a guinea pig with the profits?"

"Yeah, and Mom ended up cleaning his cage. No more lemonade stands for us."

We laugh about these and other stories.

After cleaning up the kitchen, we sit on the backyard swing. "Your parents worked hard to make this house unique," Tara says. "Their touches are everywhere. The treehouse, that fountain. The rose garden. What happens to it now that they're both gone?"

"Well, I made a decision not to make a decision."

"Um, you'll have to explain that one."

"You and others advised me not to make big moves right away. I put selling the house in that category. I'm keeping it—for now."

"Good for you, Ella."

"I do worry about Will's reaction. He wants it sold."

"Why is that a concern? It's your house, not his."

I watch birds take a bath in the fountain. "You know my husband. He likes calling the shots."

"You mean he likes to control everything—including you!"

"I have to try, Tara."

"Try and what? Be miserable?"

I ignore the jab. "Will has a right to his opinion, and so do I. I'm telling him about the house when he gets back."

"He'll be pissed. Then what?"

I hand her the two trusts, hoping to extricate myself from this rabbit hole. "Remember how I met with Mom's attorney?"

"Yes, and I know what you're doing."

"Can we please focus on the estate? I need advice."

Tara reluctantly gestures for me to continue.

I tell her about the meeting with Mr. Abrams. "I had no idea my parents accumulated such wealth. I'm unsure what to make of it."

"This is terrific news, Ella! The windfall gives you independence." Tara thumbs through the documents. "The first trust is straightforward, passing everything to you. The house has no mortgage but must be assessed for tax purposes. You'll need to file a final IRS return on Margaret's behalf."

She continues flipping pages. "The lawyer retained an investment group to manage the money. I've worked with them on several cases. They're solid."

Tara holds up the Charitable Trust. "This was a thoughtful, savvy business move on Margaret's part. I'm impressed."

"Will's upset we didn't get the money."

"That surprises you?" Tara piles both trusts on the table. "Margaret gets to say where her money goes."

"I agree."

"And you decide what to do with the inheritance. By law, Will has no right to it. Don't commingle the trust's assets with your marital assets. Otherwise, they become joint property."

"Am I making the right decision to keep the house?"

Tara sighs. "Look, I'll make this easy for you. Repeat after me. When in doubt…" She motions for me to repeat.

I play along. "When in doubt…"

"Don't."

I chuckle. "That's solid legal advice."

"Now, say the whole sentence aloud. With confidence."

I press my shoulders back in mock compliance. "When in doubt, don't!"

We erupt in laughter.

"Ella, in all seriousness, you've been through a lot. Take time to grieve. There's no rush to sell. The house isn't going anywhere."

Tara speaks wisely as a friend and lawyer. I must quit doubting myself.

"Make no major moves while you're on leave," Tara continues. "A forced timeline allows you to think rationally."

"Delay decisions for six weeks?"

"Yes. And don't commingle your inheritance. I can't emphasize it enough."

"No commingling. Got it."

She wiggles my pinkie. "Can we return to Will?"

My bestie is determined to be heard like a preacher on Sunday morning. "Before you say anything, please know I had insights about him."

"Such as?"

"He's self-serving and his love is conditional."

"You think?" Tara rolls her eyes.

"I want to find a way to communicate without him over-powering me."

"Good luck with that." She snorts. "Do you even know where he goes at night? I bet he didn't tell you I saw him at the Player's Sports Bar in the City two weeks ago."

"No, but he often entertains clients."

"Yeah, right. Let's just say I caught him having a good time. He's a narcissist, Ella. Open your eyes."

I cringe. *Mom used that exact word to describe him.*

Tara stands, pulling me up. "Enough about the evil one. Let's go read those journals. I want to see what Margaret wrote about us."

For the rest of the evening, we have an old-fashioned slumber party. We scan the journals, cook dinner, watch a movie, and eat popcorn in bed. A perfect ending to a wonderful day.

The next morning, Tara dresses in a power suit. I love watching her morph from my sidekick into a crusader for justice.

"Well, I better get a move on. Busy day." Tara picks up her bag. "July 10th is only two weeks away."

"Don't feel like celebrating this year."

"Girl, it's your thirtieth birthday." Tara winks. "We're doing something special." She has one foot out the door. "Call if things get tense with Will. I mean it, Ella. Don't let him bully you. Stand your ground."

She had to sling one last zinger before heading out to save the world.

TEN

After three soul-searching days, I have peace about not selling my childhood home. Now I have to sell the idea to a salesman. While driving to SFO, I rehearse my spiel. According to the Internet, Bay Area real estate will continue to rise in value. Mom's place is located in an exclusive neighborhood. Rent will cover its maintenance and generate a substantial income. Will gets the cash for his toys; I keep the house, a true win-win.

Yikes. Traffic on the Bay Bridge is bumper-to-bumper. Good thing I left early. One time I was late and Will gave me the silent treatment for two days. I haven't heard from him since he left. I think it's odd for couples not to check in with each other when they're apart, but what do I know?

Whoosh! A motorcycle whips past, making me jump. I hope he doesn't end up in the ER. I fight my way over to the right-hand lane and exit the freeway, tapping my fingers on the steering wheel. Twenty minutes until his plane lands. It's going to be tight.

The man of the hour refuses to wait curbside with the riffraff (his word, not mine), preferring a meet-and-greet. I park in the airport garage and set a bag of Jelly Belly candies on his seat, an expected welcome home gift.

I zigzag around people who are leaving the terminal and make my way to the electronic flight board. Oh, good. His plane just landed. I hurry to the waiting area, keeping my eyes glued on the crowd so I don't miss him.

Even though Will never finished college, his intelligence and charisma have carried him far. He earns a six-figure salary working as a sales manager for a nationwide wine distribution company. The customer in Oregon owns a restaurant chain across fourteen states, making this a lucrative account. I hope Will comes home with a signed contract. Otherwise, watch out. Six months ago, he lost a major account and ripped a flat-screen TV from our living room wall. He doesn't take rejection well.

Speaking of the devil…

Most people blend into a crowd. Not William Walker. He has a presence—tall, good-looking, affable—that makes him stand out. He acknowledges my waive with a nod, says something to his team, then cuts over to me, pulling a roller bag.

"Hey, babe." He pecks my lips. "Miss me?"

"Of course. Ready to go?"

"I've had enough of those Bozos." He tosses one last smile at his mates and drapes an arm over my shoulder. "What's my treat?"

On the ride home, Will tells me about his trip as he munches jelly beans. He sealed the deal, putting him in a fantastic mood. He's already planning a return trip to play golf with the company's CEO.

When I pull into our driveway, I flinch at the newspapers. I should've stopped by earlier to clean up.

Will notices them, also. He walks inside the house and looks around. "Papers out front, dishes in the sink, clothes on the couch."

He parks his suitcase against a wall. "You haven't stayed here since I left. Why?"

He shoots me a look that feels like a slap across the face.

"Ella, I asked a question. Answer it."

"I, uh… I stayed at Mom's. I also took a leave from my job. I'm not feeling—"

He holds up a hand to silence me. "I get it. You're not working. Why'd you stay in Piedmont?"

Deep breath. You got this. "I wasn't sure about selling the house so I spent time there. I've come up with an idea that benefits both of us."

His nostrils flare like a snake ready to strike. "Don't stop. You're on a roll."

Here goes nothing. "Instead of selling the property, we keep it. I'll find good tenants, rent it for thirty-five hundred a month, possibly more. The house pays for itself and keeps appreciating. Think of it as an investment in our future. You can have the rental income to spend any way you want. Thoughts?"

Will doesn't respond. Instead, he walks to the kitchen, opens the refrigerator, and takes out a beer. He pops the top, eyeing me as he guzzles it down. He sets the empty bottle on the counter. "This isn't what we agreed to and you know it."

He kicks off his shoes. "We'll talk about your brilliant idea later. Right now, it's time to welcome me home. Let's take a shower."

A shower? Now?

He grabs my arm and drags me down the hallway.

"Will, please! I have more to say!"

"Hush. No talk." His voice is as frosty as his eyes. Once we're in the bathroom, he strips away my clothes, shoves me into the stall, and turns on the water.

"It's freezing, Will!" I'm shivering so badly my teeth chatter.

"You'll warm up soon." He hands me a bar of soap. "Wash yourself. Everywhere."

He undresses in front of the shower door, blocking any escape. Once he's naked, he stands there pleasuring himself, watching me. He steps in and spins me around, pressing my cheek against a wall. He has me pinned; I can't move.

"Will, stop! You're hurting me!"

He yanks the soap from my hand. "Let's have some fun." He bends me over, lathers my bottom, and thrusts into me, moving slowly at first, then picking up the pace, faster and faster, race-car speed. I'm on fire; the pain is excruciating. He's pummeling me like a jackhammer. Am I screaming? I feel as if I'm screaming but Will doesn't react so maybe the sound is only in my mind. I don't know. I lose all sense of reality as the vicious assault continues.

After climaxing, he holds my head against the tile for several seconds, then releases me. He shuts off the water and steps out of the stall. I slide to the floor, sobbing, blood trickling down my leg.

"Cut the drama, Ella. It's not as if we've never done that before." He dries off, drops the towel on the floor, and saunters away.

I am numb and heartbroken. Will crossed a line. He has taken us down a dark path where monsters live and evil lurks, a place of no return. My husband raped me.

Do I call the police? Have him arrested? We have experimented but never so violently. He'll deny he forced me. It's his word against mine, fodder for neighborhood gossip if a police car shows up.

Will returns to the bathroom fully dressed. "Uh, are you okay? Guess I got carried away." He hands me a towel, avoiding eye contact.

He looks subdued, contrite. I doubt he'll hurt me again tonight because he feels guilty. But what about tomorrow? Or the day after? What happens the next time I say or do something that angers him?

ELEVEN

"Wake up, sleepy girl." Will sets a tray containing Cheerios, toast, and tea in front of me and opens the curtains to let in the morning light. "I have news to share."

I want to dump the peace offering on the floor.

"My realtor thinks we'll get a million for Piedmont, more if we create a bidding war. I have my eye on a place in Sausalito." He forces me to look at pictures on his phone from a real estate website.

"Check out the entertainment area." He enlarges a picture of a stylish outdoor kitchen with a fireplace and wicker furniture, leading to a dock. "The sailboat is included. Blows you away, doesn't it, babe?"

Unbelievable. I'm sore from the rape and he's talking about buying a new home. At least I know why he's pushing to sell Mom's house. I shiver when I realize what he's also doing: normalizing the rape by not talking about it. I gave him a pass last night. Not today.

I set the tray aside, praying he doesn't drag me into the shower again. If he does, I'll scream until my lungs burst. "How can you act so nonchalant?"

He takes a bite of toast. "I have no idea what you're talking about."

"What happened yesterday wasn't consensual, Will. You hurt me."

"That again?" He waves away my words. "Can't a guy have a little fun with his wife?"

"Forcing yourself on me wasn't fun and you know it."

"Loosen up, Ella. It's roleplay. Spices up our marriage."

I start to respond but stop. What's the use? He's delusional. If I continue pressing, he may get violent. How do I stall for time to figure out how to leave him? *Think, Ella, think...*

"I have a favor. Can we put the real estate discussion on hold until after my birthday?"

"Not happening. We need to act fast or we'll lose that waterfront gem. We should list this house, too. Gives us more leverage."

Don't react, appeal to his ego. "The homes in Sausalito are beautiful. It'd be a nice place to live."

He's listening so I talk fast, making up a story as I go. "But Piedmont's my childhood home, Will. Think about what that means to me. Maybe if I had a way to say goodbye—invite friends and neighbors over to the house—letting go of it might be easier. Plus, we can announce we're selling, creating buzz. Free marketing."

He cocks his head, sizing me up.

"It's my thirtieth birthday. Let me throw a party for myself. Your gift to me."

"A gift, huh?" He drags his finger up my inner thigh. "How can I deny my *fun-loving* wife anything?"

His sinister tone sends chills down my spine. I push his hand away, struggling to keep my voice even. "I probably should go over there tomorrow to get started on repairs. I noticed a cracked window and several doors that stick. We want top dollar."

He slides off the bed and towers over me. "Fine, but no more games, Ella. I mean it. Don't piss me off again. We're selling both houses and moving. That's the end of it."

For the rest of the day, Will watches TV and talks with his realtor. I do chores, pretending everything is normal. During dinner, he talks nonstop about my inheritance. His words sound like *blah, blah, blah.* Last night taught me he'll stop at nothing to get what he wants. Tara will guide me out of this living nightmare.

TWELVE

It's Sunday, and my insides are shaking like a seven-magnitude quake. Thankfully, a Giants game starts on ESPN in an hour. Nothing prevents Will from watching his home team play ball. Once the players are on the field, I bring him a grilled ham and cheese sandwich and a beer so he focuses on food instead of me.

"Can I get you anything else before I go?"

His eyes remain glued to the television as he takes the plate and bottle. "What time will you be back?"

Hopefully never. "Around five."

"Don't be late. I want… Damn! That idiot couldn't catch a ball if it dropped in his lap!" He bites into the sandwich.

"Will? You were saying?"

He waves me away, a pesky fly bothering him.

I jump in the car and drive off, my pulse thumping as I call Tara. *Pick-up, pick-up, pick-up.*

"Hey, girl! Ready for another—"

"Can you meet me at Mom's?"

"It's Will, isn't it? You told him about the house."

"Yes, and I need your help."

"I'm leaving now."

Tara is sitting on the front porch holding a wine bottle as I pull into the driveway. She stands. "I'm guessing the conversation with the evil one didn't go well."

"No sarcasm, please." I struggle with the lock.

"Hey, I'm sorry." Tara takes the key and opens the door. I toss my purse on a table and find tissues along the way to the backyard. Two gray squirrels are clinging to a tree, twitching their tails and screeching at each other. One races down the trunk; the other follows in hot pursuit. *Run, baby, run. Don't let him catch you.* They leap to a second tree and disappear over a fence.

Tara arrives, holding two wine glasses. She passes one over and sits next to me. "Now, tell me what's going on."

I pull my knees to my chin. "I'm such a fool for thinking he'd listen."

"Ella?" Tara gingerly touches my arm. "What happened?"

I brush away tears. "He raped me." I describe the shower incident, not holding anything back. I tell her about the house in Sausalito and the fake party. "I'm sorry for dragging you into this but didn't know where else to turn."

Tara's face turns sunburn-red. "Did you call the police?"

"No. I just want to get away."

She drinks half of her wine, then sets the glass down. "I'll be right back."

She's leaving? Now?

Tara returns, handing me a brochure. "Do you want to go to Italy? My treat."

Huh?

"I found a Tuscany spa tour to celebrate your birthday. I'd planned on taking you there in late August. The timeline just changed. We're leaving now."

My life is falling apart and she wants to go to a spa?

"You must distance yourself from him, Ella. He's too dangerous, and you're too vulnerable. You came to me for help; this is what it looks like."

I stare at the brochure. Italy. On the other side of the world. An ocean away.

"Think about Margaret's journals," Tara urges. "Italy was a nurturing place for her; it can be for you, too. Let's do this for your mom."

Her words snap me out of a dark, hopeless place. "What about Will? He'll never let me go."

"Screw him! He's lucky you're not pressing charges!" She closes her eyes and counts to ten. "He thinks the party is when? Sunday, July tenth?"

I nod.

"Let's leverage that lie to our advantage." Tara gets on the phone with her travel agent. She's wheeling and dealing, talking so fast I can't keep up.

"Great news!" she announces after ending the call. "I booked us on a tour that starts July ninth. My agent will arrange flights once I give her a departure date. We'll leave as soon as I clear my schedule. Meanwhile, you stay in the studio apartment above my office."

Tara is moving too fast. Her plan feels daunting, unmanageable, unrealistic. She's not thinking about loose ends. "There's no way we can organize a trip like this so fast."

"Let me worry about the details; you focus on healing. This vacation buys you time to wrap your head around what that bastard did to you."

I gaze at the water trickling in the fountain, such a soothing sound. A monarch butterfly flits from bloom to bloom on a lilac bush, sampling its nectar. Nature. Healing. Time. Running away to Italy does give me breathing room, a chance to clear my foggy brain. "Are you sure we can pull it off?"

She waves the brochure. "We're halfway there."

"Okay, I'll go. But we're not leaving early. I know how busy you are. Besides, I need a passport. I'll stay in Mill Valley so Will doesn't cause trouble."

"No way, Ella. You're not returning to that hellhole."

I swallow a couple of times, forcing out a painful truth. "Will punished me because I didn't follow orders. He leaves me alone if I don't challenge him."

The color drains from Tara's face. "I've waited so long for you to admit that. Now all I feel is sick to my stomach."

"There's no reason to hide the truth anymore. Not after yesterday."

Tara stares at her wine glass, swirling the amber liquid. "If he *ever* hurts you again, I'll personally drag his sorry ass to jail."

We exchange a look of mutual understanding.

"Okay, let's do this." She holds up her glass for a toast. "To best friends sneaking off to Europe. If we get caught, you're Thelma and I'm Louise."

Only Tara Marie Collins can make me feel hopeful at a time like this.

THIRTEEN

Tara and I conspire over the next hour to form a plan. She will act as my bank so I don't leave a paper trail. We create a fake to-do list for my fake party. I also identify real items around the house that need repair. Mom's long illness took a toll on the property.

We identify other things I must do: order an expedited passport, prepay the gardener, stop Mom's mail, change the alarm code, and drop off my luggage at Tara's loft ahead of time.

"Lie low," she cautions. "Everything will work out if we stick with the plan."

My insides twist into a giant pretzel as we go our separate ways. I hope this plan of hers doesn't backfire.

Will is still watching TV when I return home. I show him the lists to avert suspicion. He waves them away. "Your party, your headache. Don't drag me into it."

I'm surprised he doesn't scrutinize the details but say nothing. I'm lying low.

Tara checks on me daily while tying up loose ends. I hold my breath when Will comes home at night, hoping he hasn't discovered the ruse. I do nothing to upset him. If he's late, I praise him for working hard. I prepare gourmet food. The house is spotless, his laundry folded and put away. He's never been happier; I've never been more miserable. Knowing this sacrifice is buying Tara time keeps me sane.

Unfortunately, the only flight that gets us to our destination on time departs at seven in the morning from SFO. The evening before our escape, an invisible vice squeezes my chest as Will and I watch TV through the eleven o'clock news. We go to bed; I remain awake, waiting for him to fall asleep. Twenty minutes after his muscles relax and his breathing slows, I make my move. This moment is the most dangerous. If he wakes, I'm a goner. I tiptoe from the room and place a note Tara wrote to him on his desk. I have no idea what it says and don't care.

I'm sweating bullets as I rush from the house in my pajamas, hop in the car, and speed away. I slide off my wedding ring, dropping it in the ashtray. I want no physical reminder of my marriage. I scamper up the steps to Tara's San Francisco loft and change into my travel clothes.

A shuttle appears at 3:45 a.m. and whisks us to the airport where we walk around, sipping hot drinks. I glance over my shoulder, half-expecting Will or one of his buddies to appear.

"He tracks my phone!" I grab Tara's arm. "What if he comes to—"

"He'll never get past security." She adjusts the privacy setting and turns the phone off. "And now he can't track you."

At 7:09 a.m., the engines reverberate throughout the plane as it taxies down the runway. When the jet's thrust pushes me into the seat, my eyes pool with happy tears. Will can't touch me now.

We land in Chicago and catch an overseas flight, arriving in Florence, Italy—twenty hours after leaving home. From there, we take a train to our final destination: Montecatini. On pure adrenaline, we walk from the station to our hotel, The Tuscany Castle. Upon seeing it, we get the giggles, partly from exhaustion, and partly because our castle is a budget hotel with a gaudy façade, nothing as we imagined.

"You and I must be the king's stepchildren," Tara jokes.

Our room has twin beds, an oddly oversized bathroom, and a city view. We have two hours until we attend a tour-group reception. Tara crawls into bed and sleeps. After showering, I turn on my phone. Will has sent a dozen profanity rants, each one worse than the last. His words transport me to the shower, making me shiver.

Tiny whistles escape from Tara's mouth. She's sacrificed a lot to bring me here, both in time and money. I can either let Will terrorize me from six thousand miles away, or not. It's my choice.

I delete his texts as fast as I can. Delete, delete, delete. If others arrive, I'll get rid of those, too. I refuse to allow his threats to crawl inside my head. He is not ruining this special time with Tara.

FOURTEEN

"Ella, wake up." Tara shakes my shoulder. "We're in Montecatini and have ten minutes until the reception."

"Ugh, go away." I'm tired, disoriented, and want to sleep.

She pinches my toe on her way to the bathroom.

I reluctantly get ready and we go downstairs, arriving as the tour leader begins talking. Sabra is a thirty-something woman who dresses with flair. She's wearing a gray and yellow tunic top over black leggings with stylish sandals. Her hair and makeup look salon-worthy.

Sabra plies us with wine, provides an overview of the next nine days, then initiates an icebreaker. Each of us must interview two fellow travelers and introduce them to the group. I'm eyeing the exit door when a woman approaches me. "Hello, there! I'm Lauren. Shall we get this over with?"

Lauren is a petite, thirty-three-year-old, single lady from Texas who is also traveling with a girlfriend. Her light blond hair, clear blue eyes, and buoyant personality ooze confidence. She's a veterinarian who cares for large animals such as cows and horses. I connect with her instantly.

Once she and I finish chatting, I interview a soft-spoken man named Ryan. He's a physician assistant who works with three Internists in Idaho. He is traveling alone and talks less than me.

Sabra taps a spoon against a glass to begin the introductions. Everyone on the tour is from the United States. Two older women, who have been best friends for fifty years, brought their grown daughters. There are four girlfriend duos, two married couples, and Ryan, the only solo traveler.

We eat dinner, and by nine-thirty, the festivities conclude with Sabra wishing us *buona sera*.

Tara unlocks our door, yawing "Glad that's over."

"You and me both."

She throws on a Berkeley Law T-shirt, does her bathroom routine, and slides into bed. When I return from brushing my teeth, she's sleeping. "Good night, dear friend. Thanks for bringing me here."

I check my phone. Three more hate-filled texts from Will. Delete, delete, delete. The phone is off for good. I plug in a nightlight, recheck the door's lock, and crawl under the covers. Some people might find this old hotel's groans, pings, and whistles irritating. For me, they are the sound of safety, lulling me to sleep.

FIFTEEN

"*Buon giorno!*" Tara calls out, already showered and dressed. "We have a day to conquer, birthday girl!"

I force my eyes open. "You better not embarrass me, Tara Marie Collins. I mean it. Don't make a big deal out of today."

"Who me? Embarrass you? Never!"

We both laugh at that lie.

Thirty minutes later, I'm filling a plate with scrambled eggs, juicy strawberries, and a croissant. I'd prefer eating at a table for two but Tara sits with people from our travel group. I focus on my meal as she inserts herself into their conversations.

Sabra steps into the dining room wearing a black floppy hat and an ankle-length aqua dress that's accessorized with matching jewelry. "*Buon giorno.* The walking tour begins in fifteen minutes. Please don't be late. *Grazie.*" Our guide is not only a style maven but she rules with an iron fist.

We finish eating and walk outside, gathering in front of the hotel. Sabra completes a headcount then smiles. "Thank you for being on time, and welcome again to Montecatini Terme, Tuscany's most famous spa town. Visitors have revered its curative waters since the sixteenth century. Today, we explore it. Please follow me." She holds up a stick with a green flag and starts walking.

We pass a hand-carved merry-go-round, an Opera House, and several apartment buildings. Children wearing uniforms are hurrying up the street. Two gray-haired men sit quietly on a bench, smoking cigarettes.

Sabra assembles us in front of an impressive art deco building. "This spa is called Terme Tettuccio. People come here to ingest the mineral waters that bubble up from natural springs. It does not offer massages, baths, or other treatments like the one you will visit this afternoon."

"Woo-hoo!" shouts Lauren. "Can't wait!" She is not shy.

Sabra finishes her speech about the town's history then releases us to explore it on our own and to eat lunch.

Tara and I wander around, taking pictures of ornate water fountains. We stop at an ATM to load up on euros then find a *trattoria,* ordering pasta, salad, bread, and Chianti. We stop at a *gelateria* and have our first Italian gelato: pistachio for me, dark chocolate for her. We stroll toward our hotel, savoring each creamy bite.

At two o'clock, the tour group climbs into a bus, jockeying for front seats. Sabra waits until everyone is on board then says, "I'd like to introduce Stefano, our driver. When he's not transporting tour groups, you will find him on a soccer field."

Stefano waves, revealing a lustrous smile along with olive-green eyes, a two-day beard, and collar-length, wavy hair.

"I think I'm in love," Tara announces, her mouth gaping.

I chuckle. The power attorney looks like a smitten teen.

"I have an announcement," Sabra says with a sly smile. "Would Ella please raise her hand?"

Ugg. The dreaded moment has arrived. Up goes my reluctant arm.

"Today is Ella's birthday! Please join me in singing the famous song to her."

Tara gets a poke for whispering in Sabra's ear. It's uncomfortable having these strangers stare at me. I'm relieved when Stefano fires up the engine and drives away.

Soon, we're in Monsummano, a town surrounded by lush, rolling hills. Stefano turns onto a long driveway and stops in front of the Grotta Palatino Spa. Sabra passes out brochures. "Today, you choose your first treatment and soak in the thermal pool."

Excitement builds as everyone studies the list. "The aromatherapy facial is calling my name," Tara says. "What about you?"

"I think I'll start with a full body massage."

We pile off the bus and follow Sabra inside the spa, which is as quiet and reverent as a church. We amble down a wide corridor where decorative wall sconces cast pale-blue light, creating a mystical vibe.

We register for our treatments and wait in the lobby. One by one, people from our group disappear down interconnected corridors. An attendant calls my name, handing me a bag containing a mint-green robe, matching slippers, an orange, and a water bottle.

"Enjoy every minute," Tara says as we part ways. "We'll catch up by the pool."

I nod, giddy with anticipation over what's to come.

SIXTEEN

Instead of taking me directly to a massage room, the attendant leads me to a private room that has a twin bed, a tiny sink, and a nine-inch closet. The mini condo is mine today as part of the travel package. What an unexpected luxury!

I undress, splash cool water on my face, then lie on the bed, listening to piped-in music. A classical piece transports me to a contented place, tension leaving my body.

When it's time for my treatment, I shuffle to the lobby in my robe and slippers. A masseuse calls my name; I follow her to a massage room. Lavender—my favorite scent—floats in the air. Soothing music plays, candles flickering to its rhythm.

The woman communicates with gestures since she doesn't speak English. She steps outside the door so I can disrobe and lie face down on the massage table. It's awkward not covering up with a sheet but I go with the flow, closing my eyes and mentally visiting the Marin Headlands as a distraction.

The door opens and closes. The masseuse moves around, getting things ready. Soon, her hands touch my body with warm, lavender-scented oil. Fingers glide around my neck, over my back, around my arms and palms, across my bottom, down each leg, and ending with my feet.

Her hands never leave me as she returns to the starting point, detailing each section. Sometimes she uses light pressure. Other times, it's more intense. She senses what I need and delivers it. When she finds a knot, she massages it away. If the oil cools, she warms it. She's painting a masterpiece; I'm her canvas. Her touch is comforting, sensual, appreciated.

She gestures for me to roll over. I no longer care about my nakedness. The masseuse's skillful touch is my only focal point. She begins with the back of my neck and moves to my shoulders, arms, and hands, stretching each finger until my knuckle pops. She warms her hands with oil then slides them over my breasts and belly, down my legs, and ends with my feet.

She returns to where she started, rubbing each place in longer increments. When she reaches my thighs, sexual energy sparks. I'm floating among the stars, transcending the universe.

A tear trickles down my face from the unexpected pleasure. If the masseuse notices, she says nothing while continuing her rhythmic moves. My body responds to her touch; I'm safe like a caterpillar inside its cocoon.

She applies stronger pressure to the bottom of my feet, then finds her way to my face and scalp. Her fingertips move in tandem with my breathing. Goosebumps arrive, not because I'm cold, but from my nerve endings responding to her touch.

She ends the session with a final, gentle sweep over my entire body, slowly dragging her hands away. She sets a cup of water on a table, says something in Italian, and leaves the room.

I don't move right away, trying to understand what happened. This stranger made me feel whole and respected, filling me with sensuality. How was this possible?

SEVENTEEN

I return to my private room with a startling realization about my marriage. Will and I have sex but we're not intimate—not even on good days.

We rarely discuss thoughts and ideas. I can't remember the last time we sat and had a leisurely conversation without a TV blaring. We don't have inside jokes or have fun as a couple. We're not playful with each other. Ours is a transactional partnership where we have unspoken rules and keep score. I bet he doesn't know I have a mole on my left hip. That massage therapist could probably find it blindfolded.

I yearn for a deeper, two-way connection that fosters closeness, trust, and respect. Even if Will agrees to attend couple therapy, I doubt he can change his behavior, given his past. When kids grow up without a father and have a mother who chooses a bottle over her family, they have no role model to show them what a healthy relationship looks like.

Yikes! I've been here for almost an hour. Tara must be wondering where I am. I tug on a one-piece swimsuit and go outside to find her.

She is soaking in the thermal pool with Ryan, the man I interviewed the first night.

"It's about time!" Tara shouts. "Where've you been?"

"Enjoying my condo. How's the water?"

"It's great, Ella," Ryan says. "Come join us."

I toss my robe on a chaise lounge and step into the water. Nature's bathtub feels heavenly. An underground spring feeds the pool so it has no chlorine or other chemicals to irritate the skin. Tara, Ryan, and I float on our backs, soaking up the rays. Tara gets out to dry off, leaving Ryan and me alone.

"What treatment did you have, Ella?"

"The ninety-minute massage. You?"

"The same. Happy birthday, by the way. How many candles are on your cake?"

"Thirty. I'm starting a new decade."

"I've survived that milestone for three years. I wonder if—"

"Help!" yells a girl from our tour group. "Something's wrong with my mom!"

Ryan swims toward the pool's steps, motioning for me to follow. He kneels beside the woman, searching for a pulse. "What's wrong, Mary?"

"I'm shaky," she whispers. "Diabetic."

"Have you taken your meds? Eat anything unusual?"

"Took extra insulin this morning after eating a danish." She breaks eye contact. "Two, if I'm honest."

Ryan and I look at each other and mouth the word hypoglycemia at the same time. Mary's blood sugar has dropped and needs to be leveled. Ryan shouts, "Does anyone have orange juice or regular soda?"

A man from our group hands him a Coca-Cola. Ryan has Mary sip the drink while I run to the café to get her a protein snack.

Once Mary eats a peanut butter sandwich, her shaking subsides. I take her pulse, happy to find it normal. "How are you feeling?"

"Mostly embarrassed. I've been a diabetic for years and know better. It won't happen again."

Sabra waves Ryan and me over, confiding she's worried about Mary's health. "I'm responsible for the group's well-being." She holds up her phone. "Should I call a doctor?"

Ryan and I shake our heads. He explains hypoglycemia, and after talking with Mary, Sabra decides to leave well enough alone.

Later that afternoon, Ryan and I float in the pool again, swapping work-related stories. Tara swims up, playfully splashing us. "Are you two talking about how you saved Mary's life?"

Ryan returns her splash. "We medical types are never off the clock."

"How come you're here by yourself, Ryan?"

"You don't have to answer her nosy question," I tell him. "Tara's used to grilling people on the witness stand."

"If you must know, my fiancée left me at the altar five days ago. Italy was supposed to be our honeymoon." He dips underwater and comes up for air. "I think I'll work on my tan." He swims away and gets out of the pool.

Tara covers her face. "I blew that one."

Yes, you did. I'm tempted to apologize to Ryan on Tara's behalf. I wonder how he'd feel if he knew he wasn't the only one in our group with relationship issues?

EIGHTEEN

Tara and I return to our room that evening, feeling like wet noodles. We eat dinner at the hotel and call it a night. We need lots of energy for what Sabra has planned for us over the upcoming week.

On day three, we visit Florence, a historic city overrun with tourists. I fall in love with its famous square, Piazza Della Signoria. Sabra arranges for a guided tour of the Uffizi Gallery, one of the most renowned art museums in the Western world. Visiting these two places reminds me of the E. M. Forster novel, *A Room with a View* where George Emerson carries Lucy Honeychurch to "some steps in the Uffizi Arcade" where she faints after witnessing a stabbing in the Piazza Della Signoria. That passage sure came alive for me.

The Basilica di Santa Maria del Fiore, an immense Gothic cathedral, mesmerizes me with its sheer size, green and pink marble, and elaborately carved doors. How are humans able to create such beauty? My neck gets stiff from staring up at Brunelleschi's dome, a construction masterpiece.

I'm surrounded by ornate bridges, shopping, gelato, savory food, and art. I still can't believe I saw Michelangelo's David! Six hours is not enough time to explore this fascinating city.

Day four takes us to Pisa. The Piazza del Duomo is a wide walking area in the heart of the city. Four religious edifices dominate it: the Duomo, or cathedral, the Campanile, a free-standing bell tower better known as the Leaning Tower, the Baptistery, and the Camposanto, a walled cemetery. Tara and I can't resist taking our pictures holding up the famous tower. Who travels to Pisa and doesn't return with that photo?

On the fifth day, we visit Lucca. Its historic center, with medieval towers and nearly one hundred churches, is enclosed by a massive wall. Tara and I rent bikes and explore the city on our own. Riding through the streets with the wind in my face makes me feel like a carefree schoolgirl.

After Lucca, we travel to Collodi, a hillside village. The town is famous for one thing: Pinocchio's birthplace. My dad read stories to me about the little wooden puppet who wanted to become a real boy. We tour Pinocchio Park where the puppet's tales come alive through sculpture and mosaics. In one adventure, Pinocchio's father, Geppetto, is eaten by a whale. The park has a life-size whale sculpture, and Tara and I have our picture taken inside its mouth. What fun to be transported back to my childhood!

The last place we visit as part of the tour requires a two-hour train ride from Florence. We're visiting the Cinque Terre, a string of five villages along the rugged northern Italian coast.

From the moment we exit a dark tunnel, I know I've arrived somewhere special. The dazzling coastline and terraced hillsides are part of the Cinque Terre National Park, a UNESCO World Heritage site.

The tour group spends the day in Monterosso al Mare because of good beach access. Tara and I feel adventurous so we take a train to another village, Vernazza, for lunch. We sit by the harbor under a red umbrella eating the best wood-burning pizza I have ever tasted.

The day passes quickly, and all too soon, our group is on the train, returning to Montecatini. Most everyone is napping. Not me. Daydreaming about the Cinque Terre's azure water, hiking trails, and villages keeps me awake. What is it about this place that stirs my soul?

NINETEEN

L ast night, I dreamed about the Cinque Terre: the sea, the hill-sides, the colorful houses. Rick Steves calls it "a seductive six-mile stretch of the Italian Riviera." I'm obsessed with those five villages.

"Whatcha reading?" Tara yawns and stretches.

"Buon giorno." I hold up the guidebook. "Wish we could've stayed longer in that little piece of heaven we visited yesterday."

"Agreed."

I toss back my covers. "I need to shower. Want to use the bathroom first?"

"Naw, go for it." She unplugs her phone from the charger and scrolls through messages.

Thirty minutes later, I'm dressed and ready to go. "It's all yours."

She nods without looking up, her thumbs racing across the phone's keyboard. Managing her law practice from afar cannot be easy.

"I'm hungry. Do you mind if I go down now to eat?"

She waves me away. "I'll be there soon."

When the elevator opens, I catch my reflection on the mirrored walls. The sun has brightened my pale skin and has added golden streaks to my brown hair. My eyes are clear and sparkly. I haven't looked this healthy in a long time. I wrap my arms around my body, loving the new me. Once downstairs, I follow the aromas to the dining room and join my friends.

"We're at the spa all day, right?" Lauren stuffs green melon in her mouth.

"Uh-huh." I bite into a flaky apple pastry. "Stefano's taking us there after breakfast."

Ryan peppers an omelet. "I'm stiff from yesterday's train ride. I can't wait to soak in the grotto's steam. How about you, Ella? What are you doing?"

"I'm visiting the grotto, also, then on to a mud wrap."

"Maybe I'll try—"

Sabra interrupts our conversation, giving us the usual fifteen-minute warning. Tara dashes in behind her to wolf down breakfast.

We pile into the bus, and Stefano whisks us away. Except for yesterday, we've spent a few hours at the spa every day but it's never enough. We're ready for eight hours of pure relaxation. Tara and I beeline to the thermal pool, claiming the lounges near the café.

I work on my tan, then step into the pool and float on my back, a guilty pleasure I've come to enjoy. Ryan swims over. He's extra chatty, revealing his fiancée jilted him with the old it's-not-you-it's-me excuse. He neither saw the break-up coming nor does he understand why she waited so long to end their engagement. He says he's ready to move on but I think he has some healing to do.

We get out of the pool and dry off. Tara and Ryan drag umbrellas between our lounges for shade while I pick up lunch. "What's this heaven and hell thing people are talking about?" Tara asks when I return with turkey avocado sandwiches.

Ryan sips a cola. "The term relates to the grotto. In 1849, miners noticed steam coming from the earth and discovered a thermal cave hundreds of feet below ground. The moisturized air is supposed to detoxify you, leading to better health—unless you can't stand the hellish temperature."

"That's fascinating, Professor Ryan." Tara salutes him.

We all laugh. He has learned to take her teasing in stride.

At one o'clock, the three of us slip on robes and follow a shaded path to the grotto. We enter a dimly lit, claustrophobic cave, careful not to touch the pointy rocks.

As we move from the entrance to the deepest part of the cavern, we cross through three progressive temperature zones named after Dante's poem, *The Divine Comedy,* and its three parts: Paradiso, Purgatorio, and Inferno. The first two zones are manageable and I soak in the steam. Inferno is too hot so I pass through quickly.

The cave, with its shadows and mysteries, inspires a spiritual experience. Eight days ago, I was in Mill Valley thinking my life was over. Now, I'm limp and relaxed from thermal steam, recovering with a cup of tea in a solarium filled with tropical foliage and friends. How can a Higher Power not be guiding my life?

That evening, several of us go out to dinner. Lauren stirs the conversation with her usual humor. "Hell wiped me out! I better start living better!"

She's a fun-loving, formidable woman, both physically and mentally, a good role model for me. She married a genuine cowboy and lived on a ranch until she discovered him in bed with another woman. She booted him out and has been single ever since. Between her story, Ryan's, and mine, we could write a soap opera.

Ryan, Tara, and I walk to a *gelateria* after dinner even though we're not the least bit hungry. By now, it's a pleasant habit. We place an order and watch the chef pour a thin layer of batter onto a crepe machine. Once it's cooked to perfection, he slathers the top with hazelnut spread, folds it in half, then adds two scoops of vanilla gelato. We take the delicacy to a table, devouring it like shipwrecked orphans.

Tara smacks her lips. "Nothing will ever compare to how delicious that tasted." She tosses away our trash, and the three of us walk to the hotel.

Ryan halts just as we're about to enter the building. "Um, I'm wondering. May I steal Ella for a minute?" His eyes drift to the cobblestones. "Alone?"

Tara looks at me; I shrug, having no idea what's up.

"Go for it." Tara winks. "You kids don't stay out too late."

The night is warm and clear. I'm happy to remain outdoors longer, having fully embraced the Italian laid-back lifestyle. Ryan and I stroll down the street, soaking in the ambiance.

"This evening—the entire trip—has been incredible." Ryan waves his arm across the sky. "Full moon, new friends, the spa, ancient cities."

I rub my tummy. "And a few pounds."

He laughs. "Yeah, that, too."

Ryan sits on a bench and pats the area next to him. "I've enjoyed getting to know you, Ella. I appreciate you listening to my woes. Hope I didn't overdo it today in the pool." He stretches out his legs.

I make myself comfortable. "No worries. Not many guys open up like that. I think it shows strength. Your fiancée doesn't know what she's missing."

Ryan looks at the moon, tapping his fingers on the bench. He rotates his neck from side to side, scoots closer, and in one swift move, kisses me on the lips. "Been wanting to do that all day."

He leans in again; I push him away. "Ryan, stop. I… I'm married."

His eyes latch onto my left hand. "But you're not wearing a ring. I feel sparks when we're together. Don't you?"

"No, Ryan. It's not that way."

He picks up a pebble and tosses it several yards. "Any idea how to say awkward in Italian?"

I nudge him with my shoulder, a playful gesture to make him feel better. "No. But I know how to say friend. I'm happy to be your *amica*."

He buries his face in his hands. "And now you sound like Kaitlyn when she dumped me."

I have no idea how to respond to that one. Should I leave and give him space? Stay and talk it out?

Ryan stands, deciding for me. "We better get back before Tara calls the *polizia*."

We return to the hotel in painful silence. He walks me to the elevator, presses the button, then heads for the stairwell, taking two steps at a time. He can't get away fast enough.

I unlock my door and brace myself, expecting Tara to fire twenty questions. Instead, she's sleeping. I slide her phone from her hand and plug it into the charger without disturbing her. She's down for the night.

As I go about my nighttime routine, I can't help but think of Ryan. He's such an upstanding guy. Intelligent, kind, vulnerable. A good catch for the right woman.

I climb into bed and stare at the ceiling. Ryan has been candid with me about his personal life, yet I've said nothing to him about mine. Even worse, I hid behind my marriage tonight, pretending all is well when the opposite is true. Why hide the truth? What am I afraid of?

A heaviness weighs on me as I ponder these and other questions. It's going to be a long, sleepless night.

TWENTY

Footsteps are louder; he's closing in. Don't look back. Sprint down a dirt road, up a hill, around a corner. Faster, faster. Lungs exploding, eyes burning, rubbery legs. A hand grabs my arm and hurls me to the ground. Noooo! We're rolling, clawing, fighting—

My eyes spring open; I bolt upright, gasping for air.

A dream. It was only a dream. I'm safe in Italy with Tara. I sip water, watching the sun brighten the room. My day brain refuses to let Will hijack my thoughts but my night brain props the door open and invites him into my mind to terrorize me.

Tara doesn't have nightmares. She compartmentalizes better than anyone I know. One time, I watched her represent a client in court. She and the opposing counsel fought like bitter enemies during the trial only to go out for drinks afterward as if they were sorority sisters. She makes decisions without ever second-guessing herself. I wish I sliced through ambiguity that easily.

"Morning." Tara stretches her arms. "You're up early."

"Waiting for you to open those emeralds so I can shower."

She sticks out her leg to block my path. "Not quite yet. What's the story with Ryan?"

"Thought I dodged that bullet."

"You wish. Don't leave anything out."

I describe what transpired under the romantic Tuscany moon.

"A kiss? Really? Didn't take him long to forget his fiancée."

I shrug. "What can I say? I'm irresistible."

Tara tosses a pillow at me. I'm tempted to send two back but it's time to get moving. Except for a group dinner, we get to spend our last full day in Italy doing anything we want. Tara and I are going on a daring adventure.

Our friends are eating breakfast and sharing their plans as we arrive downstairs. Several people are returning to Florence; others are going to the spa. One couple is biking around Montecatini. Tara and I are following in my mother's footsteps.

In one of her journals, Mom wrote about a town called San Gimignano. Sabra says the journey is arduous and doesn't recommend we go. Her warning makes me anxious but doesn't deter me.

Tara and I hike to the train station. Once in Florence, we find the bus depot and buy tickets. The trip requires one transfer in a town called Poggibonsi.

We board a half-filed, double-decker bus, each claiming a window seat. The motor roars to life, leaving a trail of black smoke as it chugs down the road.

"Are we going in the right direction?" Tara says with some attitude. "Whoever heard of Poggi-woggi?"

I anticipated her sullen mood since she wanted to spend the day at the spa. Once we're out of the city, the landscape changes dramatically. Vineyards and olive groves cover the earth, a feast for the eyes. The imagery improves my travel buddy's mood immensely.

The Poggibonsi bus station is as tiny as a broom closet. No one speaks English. I'm reviewing my notes trying not to panic when a man in a rocking chair says, "You go to San Gimignano?"

I nod, noting the gray stubble poking through his chin and cheeks. "Bus come soon. You wait." He motions for us to sit nearby.

I heed the village elder's advice, and sure enough, a smaller, local bus arrives on time. My new friend gives me the OK sign; Tara and I step aboard and wave goodbye. He's such a kind man to help tourists find their way.

Twenty minutes later, the impressive San Gimignano skyline emerges. I clap my hands, unable to contain my excitement as we cruise to a stop at the town's entrance. Mom walked through these exact stone gates!

Tara and I trek over to a tourist office and pick up a map. I hand her several brochures. "Anything catch your eye?"

"Ella, it's your day. You get to choose what we do." She browses the material. "But I wouldn't mind checking out the Leonardo da Vinci Museum."

"This city is famous for its tall towers and narrow streets. I say we visit your museum then mosey around, climb a tower or two, and end up in the piazza for lunch. Maybe check out the church."

Tara chuckles. "It's nice seeing you like this."

"I'm having fun if that's what you mean."

"What I mean is you're back to your old self." She pats her back. "The travel plan worked."

I nudge her arm. "Let's go find your museum."

When you hear Leonardo da Vinci's name, famous paintings such as the *Mona Lisa* or *The Last Supper* come to mind. This museum captures his true genius. The renaissance man had his hand in everything from machinery inventions and architecture to botany, physiology, physics, philosophy, letters, and sculpture.

As we exit the museum, Tara swings her arms in the air and shouts, "The man was brilliant!" People ogle us as we hightail it down the street.

"Look!" Tara says, pointing left. "There's your tower!"

Up we climb. After a dozen or so uneven steps, the ascent gets easier. From the top, sweeping views of the landscape reward our effort. I soak in the vineyards, flowers, homes, and history, feeling like a speck of dust passing through the universe.

Hey, mom. I made it. I found my way to your special town. Did you stand in this exact spot? See what I see? I'm trying to be strong like you. I miss you so much.

Around one-thirty, hunger kicks in, so we find our way to the Piazza della Cisterna, a triangular-shaped courtyard, to search for a café.

Tara browses a menu. "I do believe it's time for a boar salami sandwich!"

"You're kidding, right?"

"Nope." She flags down a waiter who finds a table for us.

I can't imagine putting boar in my belly. I select a more sensible dish: cheese ravioli. We both have wine. And dessert, of course.

After eating, we amble through an open passage on our way to the cathedral. Tara appears sluggish as we weave past thirteen frescoes. "Are you okay?"

"Lunch isn't agreeing with me."

I take her outside for fresh air. "Let's sit in the piazza and—"

Tara sprints to nearby bushes and throws up. I pass over a tissue and find a shaded bench for her. "You need medicine to settle your stomach. Will you be okay while I search for a pharmacy?"

She gives me a weak thumbs-up.

When I return, Tara is lying on the bench with a hat covering her face. I hand her a bottle of cold water and antacids. "Keep hydrated. And take two of these. You'll feel better in no time."

While Tara rests, I focus on getting us home. I better find the right bus or we'll end up in Rome. Once I'm grounded and Tara feels better, we make our way to a bus stop across from the city's entrance. I do a happy dance when the driver confirms we're headed in the right direction.

Tara dozes most of the way home. I gaze through the window, not wanting to miss a single moment of this day. I loved San Gimignano's brick walkways, cathedral, museum, and piazza. The town is off of the beaten path with spectacular views from its many towers. I imagine that's why Mom singled it out in her journal.

The three-hour ride home gives me plenty of time to think. I've been vagabonding around Italy for the past nine days, filling up on wanton pleasures—pasta, spa, touring, vino, gelato. Naturally, I'm happy. Who wouldn't be under these fantasy circumstances?

Confronting Will in a matter of hours feels daunting. Life would be easier if I filtered decisions through a black and white lens like Tara. Good versus evil, right or wrong. Instead, I see the nuances, the gray, the possibilities.

Do I give my marriage a second chance? Or has too much happened for reconciliation? Do we call it quits and go our separate ways? What's my path forward?

TWENTY-ONE

We're back at The Castle, getting ready for tonight's dinner in the Tuscany Valley. I can't think of a dreamier way to spend our last evening in Italy.

A black dress, silver necklace, and bangles call to me. I tie a brightly colored scarf I bought in Florence around my neck, and once I slip on black ballet flats, I'm ready for the festivities.

Tara checks me out. "Nice outfit. Want to dress me so I don't embarrass you?"

I sift through our clothes, cobbling together a sleeveless cotton shirt, loose-fitting linen pants, and a pair of strappy sandals. "How's this combo?"

"Love it." Tara holds up a necklace she purchased in Lucca. "Does this go?"

"Uh-huh." I help her with the clasp. "I could get used to this life-style. How about you?"

Tara finishes dressing. "Oh, I don't know. The landscape, villages, Chianti, spa, fresh pasta. Don't you think it'd get boring after a while?"

We laugh all the way to the elevator.

As we wait for our ride, I hug Tara. "Thanks for bringing me here. Best birthday ever."

"I'm proud of you, Ella. This vacation could've been a disaster given how it started. Instead, we've had a blast. And now you have a clear mind to deal with Will."

The elevator doors open and we step inside, leaving the conversation on the third floor.

The noise on the bus is extra loud as everyone shares tidbits about their day. Tara and I get many questions about our adventure.

Stefano skillfully navigates a narrow road as he climbs into the hills, passing one breathtaking view after another. Tara tugs my arm. "Check out those sunflowers. It's as if they're woven into the earth."

She rarely focuses on anything except her law practice. Watching this carefree side of her emerge makes me want to plan more trips. Traveling has been good for both of us.

Stefano turns off the main road and drives up a winding lane that ends on a hilltop in front of a stone farmhouse. Two people step outside; we gather around them.

"*Buona sera!* Welcome to our home. I am Caterina, and this is my husband, Affonso. We are your hosts for tonight's dinner. Affonso's brother, Enzo, is your chef. We promise to make your last evening in Italy memorable. *Buon divertimento!*"

Ryan sidles up beside me as I'm walking to the backyard. "You look nice, Ella."

"Thanks. Isn't this a great way to end the vacation?"

"Um, about last night..."

"You don't have to explain, Ryan."

"Yeah, I do. I acted like a jerk. I'm sorry that—"

Lauren slips in between us, locking our arms. "Did we pass through a time warp or what?"

Ryan shakes his arm free. "Enjoy your evening, ladies."

"Was it something I said?" Lauren raises a palm as Ryan walks away.

"He and I were tying loose ends."

"Is that code for exchanging phone numbers? I see how he looks at you."

I ignore Lauren's teasing. One afternoon while soaking in the pool, I told her about Will. Nothing about the abuse, only that we were drifting apart.

"All kidding aside," Lauren says, "we're flying home tomorrow. Are you ready to face your other half?"

"That's a loaded question."

"I've watched you, Ella. You've changed during this vacation. You're more relaxed, engaged. Italy's been good for you. Don't fall back into old habits—"

"Hey, you two." Tara catches up. "Why the serious faces on a night like this?"

"I was telling Ella to—"

"Race you to the antipasti!" I scurry to the backyard. These two are not ganging up on me.

"You can run but can't hide!" Lauren yells in a Texas drawl.

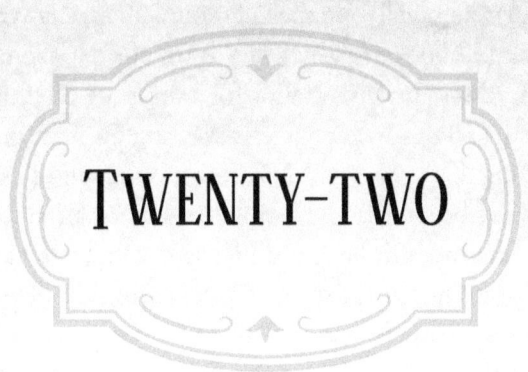

TWENTY-TWO

I t's dusk now. A striking sunset of pink, orange, and purple flashes across the sky. Acres of flowers and vineyards set the landscape ablaze with color.

Grapevines cling to trellises by the farmhouse; white lights crisscross an outdoor patio. Three tables with canary-yellow linens are pushed together for us to eat as a group. Vases overflowing with lavender serve as centerpieces, their fragrance drifting in all directions.

Affonso pours wine, sparkling water, and sangria as Italian music plays on hidden speakers. Caterina and Enzo set out platters of artichoke and sun-dried tomato bruschetta, stuffed mushrooms, marinated olives, and prosciutto for us to nibble on. I seal these images in my brain, an invisible treasure to carry home.

Sabra taps her glass with a spoon. "May I have your attention, please?"

We gather around her.

"In a minute, our hosts will serve your farewell dinner. I want to thank you for being such a wonderful group. I have enjoyed getting to know you, and I hope our paths cross again one day soon."

Everyone claps, praising Sabra for taking us on this unforgettable journey. Practically everyone is wearing an item purchased in Italy—clothing, hats, jewelry. My fellow travelers and I are no longer strangers. We've become friends—in a ten-day vacation sort of way.

Couples are more in love, mothers and daughters have renewed bonds, and girlfriends have deepened their friendships. Even Ryan has shed his sadness, ready to find love again.

We sit at the dinner table as our hosts serve warm bread, salad, seasoned chicken, and pasta with fresh tomato and basil. It's authentic Italian cuisine, delicious and plentiful.

Following the banquet, we sing and dance, creating our entertainment. I slip away to a nook that overlooks the valley. Lauren is right. I have changed since arriving in Italy. Coming here has allowed me to rediscover the woman my parents raised.

Tara intuitively guided me through a horrific situation. I shudder to think what would've happened had I stayed in California. Now, I must trust my instincts to keep the momentum going.

I catch Tara's eye; soon she's standing next to me.

"Why are you here," she asks, "when the party's elsewhere?"

"I have something to tell you." I gesture to a chair, barely able to fathom what I'm about to say. "I have two weeks before returning to work. I want to spend them in the Cinque Terre. Please don't talk me out of it."

Tara's eyes widen. "By yourself? You know I can't stay any longer."

"Earlier at the hotel, you said I have a clear mind concerning Will. That's not quite true."

"What'd you mean?"

"I'll never forget what he did to me. And we both know he has a Texas-sized ego. But he also shows up, like when Mom died."

"Oh, Ella." Tara releases a long, frustrated sigh. "Please don't tell me you're going back to him."

"Honestly? I haven't made up my mind."

"So, instead of dealing with the situation, you want to hide in the Cinque Terre? How does that move you forward?"

"I have no illusions about my marriage, Tara. Before ending it, I want to make sure it's the right decision."

"And you think staying here alone will enlighten you?"

I shrug. "Doing this feels important. Those five villages are magnets drawing me to them."

"You haven't traveled much, Ella. Staying alone in a foreign country is a big deal. There's the language barrier, getting sick, safety concerns. I could go on."

"I won't lie. I am scared. I'm even more frightened not to finish the journey you launched me on. It's grown larger than Will. I want to discover why I was put on this earth, my purpose in life. I can't do that in Mill Valley."

Tara closes her eyes, shaking her head. "You're in denial. You know who you are and what you have to do. Avoiding Will for another two weeks will only make things worse."

I clasp her hand. "I know you don't approve. And, yes, I'm running. But this time it's toward something instead of away from it. Can you understand the difference?"

"Oh, Ella. You're such a dreamer. Do what you have to do, go find your destiny or whatever. Just stay safe." She stands. "Let's go chat with Sabra about you staying."

TWENTY-THREE

We pile into Stefano's bus close to eleven, filled with food and lasting memories. At first, everyone chatters about the enchanting evening. Several miles down the road, the back-and-forth movement rocks passengers to sleep. Not me. I'm wide awake, waiting for the sign.

Sabra pats the seat next to her. She wanted to talk on the ride home to avoid interruptions. She scoots over to make room for me.

"You mentioned returning to the Cinque Terre. How may I assist you, Ella?"

"Two things. Will you help me change my flight? Recommend a place to stay in Vernazza?"

"I will cancel your air since it's part of the tour. Rebooking will cost extra so you must call."

"I understand."

"How long do you wish to stay in Vernazza?"

"Two weeks."

Sabra raises an eyebrow. "That's a long time in a small village. Maybe you want to split your time? Monterosso has much to offer."

"No, just Vernazza."

She studies my face for clues; I resist the urge to explain.

"Very well. I have contacts in the region and will call in the morning. Is there anything else?"

"No, just that." I thank her and return to my seat before changing my mind.

Tara and I rise early to pack. She has an afternoon flight out of Florence, and I have a train to catch. She hands me an envelope filled with euros and a debit card. "This will keep you going."

"You are such a generous person, Tara Collins. What would I do without you?"

She waits for a beat, then snickers. "You're about to find out."

I laugh at her well-timed joke. We finish packing, set our luggage outside the door for pick-up, and go downstairs.

Sabra finds me in the dining room and pulls me aside. *"Buon giorno,* Ella. I canceled your flight." She passes over a revised itinerary.

"And Vernazza?"

"I found an apartment near the harbor." She hands me one of her business cards where she has written a woman's name, address, and phone number. "Call me if anything goes wrong. You are not alone in my country."

I hug her as if she's a long-lost friend. "I'll always remember your kindness."

"I hope you find what you are seeking, Ella."

Sabra and I share a knowing look, one of kindred spirits. I suspect she's been on this self-discovery journey, also.

The bus ride to Florence gives the group time to exchange emails, phone numbers, and promises to stay in touch. Stefano's first stop is the train station. My pulse races as I stand and announce my plans to everyone.

"Woo-hoo!" shouts Lauren. "You go, girl! Send a postcard!"

Ryan looks very confused. I wish I had time to explain.

"I enjoyed meeting all of you. Have a safe flight home." I face Tara. "May we talk outside?" I turn to Sabra and plead, "We'll be quick."

On the sidewalk, I throw my arms around Tara, bursting into tears. "I'm fine but need one more hug. I'll miss you so much!"

"What you're doing takes guts, my friend. Promise to make each moment count."

Sabra lowers a window. "Time to go, ladies. *Buona fortuna,* Ella."

Tara whispers the debit card's security code in my ear. "Don't be afraid to use it." She steps into the bus and waves, leaving me alone to meet my destiny.

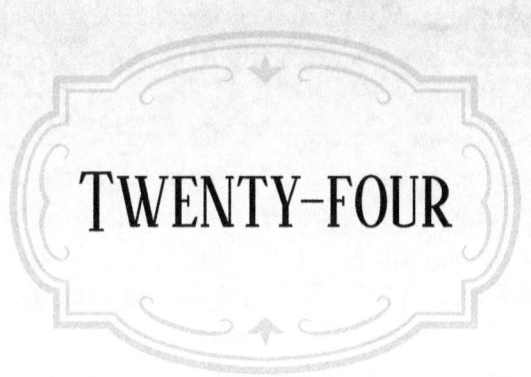

TWENTY-FOUR

I board a train for the two-hour ride to La Spezia with sweaty palms and a racing heart. I transfer to a smaller Cinque Terre train and sit by a window on the left side, knowing the thrill that awaits.

As we chug through the rock tunnel, I hover on the seat's edge. A small light gets brighter, and then *wham!* The Ligurian coastline springs from the darkness, the Mediterranean Sea nearly blinding me.

The view is magnificent, spectacular, imposing. No single word does this trance-inducing sight justice. The villages of Monterosso, Vernazza, Corniglia, Manarola, and Riomaggiore are my sanctuary for two glorious weeks. I'm giddy with excitement and nervous beyond measure.

When the train stops at Vernazza, I hike down the main street, Via Roma, until it ends at the Piazza Marconi. Using the contact information from Sabra, I locate the address and knock on a door. I rub my sweaty palms on my pants after no one answers. What if I can't reach this lady? Where will I stay?

I call the phone number on the card and cross my fingers. A woman answers in Italian. I blurt, "Sabra sent me," hoping she recognizes the name. A buzzer unlocks the door, returning my breathing to normal.

Isabella meets me in a cramped lobby with a welcoming smile. We communicate as best we can, using gestures to fill in missing words. After completing a registration card and paying for the room, she leads me through the piazza. We climb a steep rock stairway to a second-floor apartment. She shows me how to open the lock with a rusted key—it's tricky—and wishes me well.

I sure miss Tara. The room is too quiet without her. I text her about my safe arrival, sit on the lumpy mattress, and glance around.

The cramped bathroom has a shower head with no stall or curtain so the toilet, sink, and floor will get soaked every time I turn on the faucet. A scratched table holds a mini-fridge and warming plate. There's a faded leather chair next to a window; a clothesline bounces in the breeze of an alley. If I crane my neck, I see the ocean. This place is no luxury villa but it's all mine. How will I fill the days? Who will I meet? How will coming to this village change me? Those are three of many questions swirling in my mind as I curl up for an afternoon nap.

I awake to hunger pangs, a reminder I haven't eaten since breakfast. Do I find a food shop and bring dinner to the room? No, that's the easy way out. I must face my fear of eating alone in public. But first, a shower.

The water is mostly warm, never hot, and occasionally cold. I dress in my least dirty outfit and walk downstairs to a castle by the harbor that has an outdoor restaurant. Why not splurge on a fancy meal to celebrate my courage?

"*Buona sera, signorina,*" a sharply-dressed waiter says. "Will you be dining alone?"

I nod, grateful for the English. He leads me to a table and passes over a menu. "May I bring you a drink?"

My first meal alone. "A glass of red wine, please. Something from the region. You choose."

"Certainly. I will return shortly to take your order."

I study the menu, wishing Tara was here. It's odd not having her sit across from me during a meal. I press my thigh to stop it from bouncing.

The waiter sets the wine and a bread basket in front of me. "What would the *signorina* like to eat?"

"A caprese salad and spaghetti alla marinara, *per favore.*"

He nods, raising his chin toward the Mediterranean. "Enjoy the sunset."

The fruity wine smells heavenly. *Mmm…* It's delicious. The bread is warm, straight from the oven. Tara would devour it in two seconds. She'd love watching the wind send gentle waves up the coast. The birds squawking overhead would drive her insane.

I'm finishing the last piece of bread as dinner arrives. Oh my, the pasta is fresh and yummy, the tomatoes juicy, the mozzarella creamy. I eat slowly, savoring each bite. When the waiter brings the check, he sets a tiramisu in front of me.

"For the lovely *signorina.*" His smile reaches his eyes.

I devour the surprise dessert and leave a generous tip, feeling on top of the world. My first solo meal was a raging success.

A breeze carries animated conversations across the piazza. Food aromas make my mouth water even though I'm full. I stroll over to the beach, take off my sandals, and wiggle my toes in the warm water. Who knew happiness came from such simple pleasures?

Hundreds of lights link restaurants, creating a fairytale-like setting. The village is captivating during the day but at night it takes on a magical glow. I pinch myself to make sure I'm really standing here. No pressure, no expectations, no rules.

I gaze into the sky, remembering a childhood poem my dad taught me. *Star light, star bright, first star I see tonight. I wish I may, I wish I might, have this wish I wish tonight.*

Will my wishes come true?

TWENTY-FIVE

Waking up without an alarm is such a luxury. I pad over to the window and stretch my arms. I feel sad for people who sleep through dawn, that glorious transition from darkness to light when the air is crisp and the universe births a new day. The silence resets our minds, giving us a second chance.

I dress and go downstairs in search of breakfast. A tabby cat greets me about halfway down, rubbing and purring against my leg. Tara keeps a cat at her law office, a mascot that bonds her team. This furball is a friendly little thing. I'll have to bring her a treat.

Vernazza is slowly coming to life. Small vans deliver fruit, vegetables, and flowers to stores and restaurants. *Panetterias* fill the air with tempting aromas. I randomly pick one and step inside, buying artichoke *focaccia* from a hard-working baker.

"*Grazie,* Aberto." I point to his name tag when he gives me a curious stare. Why not make friends with the locals?

Instead of eating in my room, I find a bench near the harbor. It's time to push through my shyness.

Oh, my. The *focaccia's* cheese is bubbly and crusted, and the artichokes are seasoned to perfection. I lick my fingers, saving a few crumbs for that kitty. I'm definitely visiting Aberto again.

Fishing boats exit the harbor and motor out to sea. Workers hose the cobblestones, washing away last night's fun. The sun warms my face, a nudge to get moving. I visit a small grocery store called an *alimentari* to stock up on supplies then return to the apartment.

My travel book is chock-full of ideas. The trail from Vernazza to Monterosso looks interesting. The hike covers two and a half miles and has some rugged terrain, nothing I can't handle. I'll explore Monterosso, then take the train back home.

"Good plan, don't you think?" I say to the doves on my window sill. They coo and nod as if we're having a real conversation.

I pack the usual stuff—phone, water, granola bar, sunscreen, book, money—in a backpack. Once I slather on sunscreen and secure my wide-brimmed hat, I'm ready to take on the day.

I trot up to the depot to buy a Cinque Terre Card, which gives me access to walking trails, trains, and museums. With a pass in hand, I locate the red and white sign on Via Roma that points toward Monterosso and take my first step on the famous Sentiero Azzurro trail. I can't believe I'm doing this! By myself!

A steady, thirty-minute climb leads to a jaw-dropping view of Vernazza. Tiny boats float in the harbor. People are milling around the piazza, looking like ants. If I squint, I see the stairway to my apartment. There's a church with an ornate bell tower I must visit. I take several selfies but can't get a decent angle. Should I send Tara a lousy photo or ask for help? I might as well go for the gold.

"Pardon me," I say to a man and woman standing nearby. "Would you mind taking my picture?"

The man holds up a camera. "I was about to ask you the same question. We have to prove we were here, right?"

"Exactly!"

After we get our calendar-worthy photos, I press on. The trail narrows with drops of ten to fifteen feet in places with only a two-foot stone wall separating hikers from olive and lemon groves. Small houses carved into the hillside seem to defy gravity. An elderly woman stands on a balcony of one, tending a flower box. Talk about a postcard moment! Further up the trail, a farmer is transporting purple grapes down the hill using a monorail. It's such an efficient way to get crops to market.

The uneven path delivers a challenging workout made worse by the blistering sun. When perspiration dots my face, I stop under a leafy tree to rest and drink water. Once I'm reenergized, I continue climbing.

Around the corner is a glorious sight: Monterosso in the distance. Yay! I'm almost there! The trail narrows, leading to a steep stairway of several hundred, uneven steps. People pass me climbing up, struggling for breath. I made a wise decision to take the train home.

Minutes later, I spot a boy and girl, probably in their late teens, hovering over a third boy who is lying on the ground. I remember them racing past me earlier on the trail. The girl shakes the boy's shoulder. "Craig! Wake up!" She turns to the other boy. "Do something!"

These kids are in trouble. I hurry over. "Hi. I'm a nurse. What's wrong with your friend?"

"He got dizzy and fell," the girl sobs. "He won't open his eyes!"

I kneel beside him. The boy has a ninety-two pulse, dry skin, and cracked lips. He looks severely dehydrated. Not good.

"When was the last time he drank water?" I ask the girl.

"Who knows?" She grabs my arm. "Will you help him?"

"We must cool him down. Drag him under that tree and take off his shirt."

The kids follow my orders.

Other hikers have gathered, whispering. I ignore them. This boy has a life-threatening condition; I must act fast. I zip open my backpack, pull out water bottles, and sit in the dirt with the boy's head on my lap.

"Hi, Craig. I'm Ella." I pat his cheeks to rouse him. When he groans, I dribble water in his mouth. He chokes, sending the precious liquid down his chin. I prop him up and try again. This time he swallows a quarter of the bottle. I soak his shirt in water then use it to pat his face, neck, and shoulders to lower his body temperature.

More sips, more pats, more pleas. His pulse slows to seventy-eight, closer to normal. I feel such relief when his eyes flutter open. The shade, mini-bath, and hydration are working.

"Feeling better?" I ask him.

"Yeah, I think so." Craig struggles to sit up.

I maneuver him against a tree and slide the wet shirt over his chest to continue the cooling process. Color has returned to his face; his pulse is within normal limits. Crisis averted.

"Will he be okay?" The girl straightens out his shirt.

"He should be fine. His body overheated because wasn't drinking enough water. During hot days, we all need extra fluids. Hats and sunscreen also help."

I hand Craig my last bottle. "Take frequent sips. When you get to Monterosso, all three of you drink lots of water."

"We will, I promise." The girl wraps her arms around my neck. "Thanks so much for helping us! We owe you big time."

I assist Craig up, giving him a chance to steady himself. His friends stand on either side, holding his arms. "Take it slow on the way down," I caution. "And stay in the shade as much as possible."

The trio continues their descent into Monterosso. Soon, hikers are coming and going along the trail as if nothing happened.

I find a shade tree and hunker down, resting my forehead on my knees to let the adrenaline rush resolve. *Breathe in, out, in, out, in, out. Everything turned out fine, in and out, in and out.*

"Well done, Ella."

A low voice startles me. I glance up into sapphire eyes. "Have we met?"

"Not yet." He extends an arm. "I'm Jack. I watched you handle that incident from beginning to end. Very impressive. The kid was lucky you stopped."

Firm handshake. Medium height, clean-shaven, short dark hair graying at the temples.

"Thanks. I'm glad everything turned out okay."

"I noticed you gave away your water supply." He holds out a bottle. "I don't want to worry about you fainting."

His humor brings out a chuckle. "I'm almost at Monterosso—my destination." I gesture up the trail. "You'll need it more than me."

"Okay, then. I'll be on my way." He returns the bottle to his camera bag, lays a tripod over his shoulder, and starts walking. After several steps, he turns around.

"Be sure to visit the village's church, Ella. It's a real beauty."

As he continues his ascent, my heart skips a beat. Between the waiter last night and this guy, I'm walking on air. Traveling alone has its perks. I dust off my pants and wiggle into my backpack. On to Monterosso. I have a church to visit.

TWENTY-SIX

Well, I made it! Monterosso has a long, sandy beach with brightly colored umbrellas dotting the shoreline. I didn't spend much time here with the tour group. Today, that changes.

I buy a sandwich and water at a food cart called *La Scogliera,* and sit under a blue umbrella with my travel book, ticking off places to visit. After finishing my meal, I set a course for The Chiesa di San Giovanni Battista.

The fourteenth-century Catholic church is easy to find because of its dramatic horizontal black and white stripes. Or are they dark green and white? It's hard to tell. Above the door is a painting of John the Baptist along with a stunning rose-shaped, stained-glass window.

The bold stripes on the outside are replicated on pillars and arches inside the church. The rose window casts rays of diffused light, setting a spiritual tone. Jack knows his churches. This one is a beauty.

I'm walking toward the altar when a man asks visitors to vacate the premises. The reason becomes obvious as I pass a bride standing in front of the building. She's young and lovely in an ivory dress that hugs her curves. Scarlet lipstick makes her lips look like ripe berries.

Once the wedding party enters the church, I find my way to Obertenghi Castle, the village's one-time fortress. I move quickly through the ruins, visiting the ancestor tombs before hiking down to the beach.

A man wearing only Speedos lies on a boulder sunning himself, his legs draped like silk over the rock's edge. Another man lies on his portly belly in a boat that's bobbing on turquoise water. He's reading a newspaper, his hairy legs crossed at the ankles.

I want to be infected by their relaxation bug. I rent an umbrella and lounge chair, and settle in on the beach, letting my mind wander. The hike from Vernazza was beyond amazing. Helping the boy felt good. And meeting Jack with his quick wit gave me an unexpected tingle. Seeing the bride and groom was a pleasant surprise. Did I glow like her on my wedding day?

I open a novel but can't concentrate. The man next to me is rubbing sunscreen on a woman in slow, sensual strokes. He pinches her butt; she swats his hand. They're playful, in love. I bet he has never dragged her through a house and shoved her into a cold shower.

I promised to live with Will for better or worse but never imagined how bad the 'worse' could get. I suppose staying in an unhealthy relationship is easier than facing the unknown. Not anymore. Not after coming to Italy and seeing better ways to live.

When I return home, I'm filing for divorce. Why delay the inevitable? I'll never trust him again, not after what he did to me. And it's not only the abuse. His secrecy, his desire for control, and his quest for bigger and better will never end. He will always overpower me to get what he wants. I don't want to live that way.

Instead of selling Mom's house, I'm living there. Maybe I'll adopt a child as a single parent. Other women do that, right? Perhaps I'll work in another country, learn a second language. A sense of calm fills me as I consider a new direction for my life. I close my eyes and drift into the most blissful sleep.

TWENTY-SEVEN

I hike to the train station in the late afternoon, returning my dirty and tired feet to Vernazza. Swimmers in the harbor stir an idea. I hope they don't mind company. I hurry to the room, tug on a swimsuit, and return to the beach, kicking off my sandals.

The water is warm and inviting. I swim around, washing away the day's grime. A stray ball bops my head. The owner invites me to play volleyball, a conciliatory prize for my non-injury. Normally, I'd say no but this is no ordinary day. "I'd love to."

I join in the fun until my skin prunes up, then lie on a towel, letting the sun smooth out the wrinkles. In the late afternoon, hunger prods me back to my apartment. I shower, washing my body and clothes simultaneously, then hang the laundry on the outside line. How's that for efficiency? A sleeveless blue cotton dress and sandals become my dinner outfit.

It's my mission to dine at every restaurant in town. Tonight, Trattoria Gianni gets my vote. The piazza is crowded with at least double the people from last night. Maybe because of the later hour?

The restaurant host looks sympathetic when he learns I don't have a reservation. He says the wait is over an hour. Two other places give me the same unwelcome news.

Not wanting to hang around, I walk to the train station. Why not try my luck in another village? I hop aboard the first train that arrives, getting off in Manarola. Two points for spontaneity!

The village clings to the cliffs, looking as if it's about to slide into the sea. I can't wait to explore it during daylight hours. I hop off the train and walk into town. Oh, no. This village is crowded, too. I better start making reservations.

I pass several restaurants before finding one with an open table, a friendly ambiance, and a smiling host. *"Buona sera, signorina.* Are you meeting someone?"

"No, a single table, please. *Grazie."*

The waiter wrinkles his brow. "I am very sorry. There are no openings until nine-thirty. Perhaps you—"

"The *signorina* can sit with me if she wants." A man gestures to an empty chair at his table.

I recognize him immediately. He's Jack, the man who stopped to chat on the trail. "Hi, there. Nice to see you again." I fiddle with my hair. "I don't want to trouble you."

"It's no trouble at all," comes his swift reply. "Truth is, I'd enjoy the company." He stands, pulling out a chair.

Should I say yes? Make an excuse? I'm hungry enough to eat a rock. How can I go wrong with a guy who likes churches? "This is very kind of you."

He sits across from me. "Are you staying in this village, Ella?"

He remembered my name. "No, I'm in Vernazza. It's crowded tonight. Thought I'd try a different place for dinner." I hold up my pass. "This baby takes me everywhere."

Jack pulls the same pass from his shirt pocket. "I know exactly what you mean."

I unfold a napkin on my lap. "Are you staying in Manarola?"

"Nope. I'm next door in Riomaggiore."

Jack has creases around his eyes. He has a confident, easy way about him. I'm guessing he's in his late thirties. Why is he alone?

"Couldn't your family join you tonight?"

He tilts his head. "I'm traveling solo. Always wanted to photograph the Cinque Terre, so here I am."

"I remember the equipment you were carrying. Are you a professional photographer?"

He rearranges his silverware. "I strive to be."

Over pesto lasagna for me and fish stew for Jack, we chit-chat about our day while sharing a bottle of Sciacchetrà wine. It's easy to get lost in his eyes as he describes the intricacies of photography.

When the waiter brings the bill, Jack snatches it. "My treat. For rescuing that boy."

"Dining with you is my reward." I hold out thirty euros.

He gently pushes my hand away and drops a credit card on top of the bill. "I insist."

Letting him pay avoids a confrontation. Doing so, however, obligates me. Also, if a stranger can intimidate me, how will I stand up to my husband? It's time to test my mettle.

"Please. I want to pay my portion. It's important."

He waits a moment then nods, taking back his card.

We split the bill, each paying in euros.

I'm unsure if it's the fabulous meal, Jack's eyes, or the fact he let me be me, but I don't want our evening to end. I'm ready to ask if he wants to explore the town when he says, "Ella? Would you enjoy a short walk before going our separate ways?"

"You read my mind."

He smiles, not one of those flirty, toothy grins. More of a slight lifting of lips, a show of restraint.

"This village and Riomaggiore are connected by the Sentiero Azzurro trail, an easy twenty-five-minute stroll on a flat, paved path." Jack waves his pass in the air. "It's free for cardholders."

"Well? What are we waiting for?"

We amble through town, talking about this and that. As we arrive at the trail, a balmy breeze tosses my hair around. The moon glistens across the indigo water; invisible waves lap against the coastline. I get anxious upon entering a graffiti-marred tunnel and seeing a chain-link fence containing hundreds of locks. Does the Cinque Terre have a gang problem? I glance over my shoulder to see if anyone has followed us.

"Ahh, the romantics." Jack wiggles a padlock. "Couples secure these on the fence then toss the key into the water, a symbol of everlasting love."

"No key, no opening the lock. That explains one mystery. What about the graffiti?"

"Love messages." He chuckles. "Don't get any wrong ideas about me bringing you here. I wanted to show you this famous place. Or should I say infamous?"

I like his subtle humor.

"The Cinque Terre was isolated until the last century. Villagers rarely married anyone from outside their town. In the 1920s, this trail was built to connect Riomaggiore and Manarola. The area became a lovers' meeting spot."

"Hence the locks and graffiti."

"And the name. Via dell'Amore means Pathway of Love." His eyes glow. "Now you know the trail's history, courtesy of Rick Steves."

Should I tell him we follow the same travel guru? "I better hit the books so I'm able to impress you the next time we bump into each other."

We arrive at the train platform. Jack looks at his watch and down the tracks. He picks up a plastic water bottle, tossing it into a garbage bin. "Would you like there to be a next time, Ella?"

Huh?

"I'm taking a ferry to Portofino tomorrow to photograph the town and coastline. Want to come? I could use a photo assistant."

Oh, my. He's serious. "Portofino?"

"It's a village on the Italian Riviera about eighty miles up the coast. Plan on a full day."

I should say no because I barely know him, yet I feel safe. And I don't have other plans. *Carpe diem.* "That sounds fun."

He pulls out a phone and presses buttons. "I'm booked on the nine-ten ferry. It swings by Vernazza at nine-thirty. Is that too early?"

"Not at all."

He looks as happy as I feel.

A train rolls into the station, ending our time together. "Thanks for a wonderful evening, Jack. I guess I'll see you tomorrow."

"I'm looking forward to it."

I step aboard, find a seat, and glance out the window. My dinner companion hasn't moved even though he's in his home village. He returns my wave as the train leaves the station. Who is this man and why do our paths keep crossing? And why is my heart fluttering like ten hummingbird wings?

Jack wants me to be his photo assistant. Ha! He'll be disappointed to learn my camera skills begin with pointing and end with clicking. No matter. I'm visiting Portofino! Two more spontaneity points. I'm on fire!

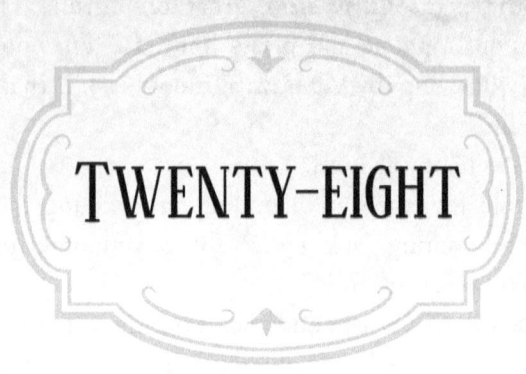

TWENTY-EIGHT

Light seeps into my room, signaling a new day in paradise. Last night's impromptu dinner with Jack plays like a movie in my mind and I watch it with glee. Twenty-four hours ago, we were strangers. Now, we're travel companions. Go figure.

I shower, then try on three outfits before finding the right combo. Aberto flashes a welcoming smile as I arrive for breakfast. *"Buon giorno, bella signorina.* What would you like to eat?"

"Buon giorno, Aberto. I'm Ella. What do you suggest?"

"I take out from oven *focaccia* with meat, cheese, and herbs, Ella."

I like how my name rolls off of his tongue. "I'll have one, please. *Grazie.*"

More locals return my wave as I stroll to the harbor to eat breakfast. *Mmm.* The food melts in my mouth. I toss crumbs to hungry pigeons. In less than an hour, the ferry will arrive, carrying a handsome photographer. Will our chemistry continue? Or was last night an anomaly?

I lick my fingers and toss my trash in the garbage. That was *deliziosa*. I return to my apartment, restock the backpack, and then scurry to the harbor to buy a ticket, lining up with other tourists.

As a ferry drifts toward Vernazza, I tent my hands above my eyes, scanning the passengers. Where are you, Jack? When a man wearing khakis and a green shirt with rolled sleeves waves, I force myself not to push past other people.

"Ready for work?" Jack helps me onboard. "You are aware assistants do the heavy lifting, right?"

"I had no idea. Are you a good teacher?"

"You can rate me at the end of the day." He hands me a water bottle. "Don't want you to get dehydrated." Those blue eyes have a mischievous twinkle.

"Won't happen with you around."

"I saved two seats up front. Is that okay?"

I nod, happy to sit anywhere as long as it's beside him.

As the ferry continues on its way, Jack is all business, fussing over camera settings and taking pictures of villages, people, and landscape. He exudes such passion. In between shots, I ask, "Where'd you learn your craft?"

He sets his camera down, sipping water. "My dad taught me."

Our banter continues as the boat meanders down the coast. I'm loving every minute with this guy. Soon, we arrive in Portofino. The town's half-moon village with its pastel houses and shops is beyond gorgeous. Boats of all sizes, including luxury yachts, are moored in the harbor.

"I see why you wanted to come here, Jack. It's pretty special."

"Agreed." He snaps several more photos. "There are three sites I want to visit. A church, a castle, and a lighthouse." He tilts his head. "What about you, Ella?" What's on your list?"

"Yesterday, this place wasn't on my radar. I'm just glad to be here." *With you.*

We're lined up to disembark when a tour group pushes past, separating Jack and me. He reaches for my hand, tugging me toward him.

His skin is warm and soft, his grip firm. He releases me once the crowd disperses. "Didn't want you to get lost in the stampede."

I'm floating on air over the way he treats me. He's nurturing, thoughtful. A sign guides us up a steep, narrow peninsula with the harbor on one side and the Ligurian Sea on the other. We arrive at a small, weather-beaten church called San Giorgio. Jack takes his photos and we check out some old paintings before continuing up the path.

At the top of the hill is a castle named Castello Brown. Jack leads us past a stone terrace to a backyard wall, overlooking the harbor and miles of pristine water. He sweeps an arm across the vista. "Can you believe this beauty?"

I smile, thinking about both the view and the man. I hold up my camera. "May I take your picture?"

He makes a silly face, making me laugh. "Tell me when you're serious." He finally poses. I can't wait to show Tara my new travel buddy.

We explore the gardens and the castle's interior, looking at decades-old, black-and-white photos of Hollywood celebrities. We continue up the hill, following signs to Il Faro.

Jack finds the lighthouse hidden behind trees and gets lost in his work. One thing is for certain: this man does not need an assistant.

A nearby food shack gives me an idea. I slip away to buy gelato, a small gesture to thank him for allowing me to tag along. *Hmm...* What flavor would he like? Vanilla is safe; you can't go wrong with chocolate. Lemon is fabulous, as is coconut. I tap my foot, trying to decide what to buy.

I laugh at myself.

Why am I getting worked up? This isn't a life-or-death decision. I order a large pistachio and stick two spoons in it. If Jack doesn't like the flavor, I'll get him something else. Problem solved.

When I return, he's waiting for me. He eyes the treat. "I wondered where you went." He picks up a spoon and samples it. *"Mmm.* This is good. How'd you know pistachio is a favorite?"

"Lucky guess."

We sit on a bench, savoring the frozen dessert. My comfort level with Jack is simply unexplainable. It's as if we've known each other for months instead of a day. For reasons I can't explain, we go together like sleep and dreams.

He feeds me the last bite, looking as if he wants to kiss me.

I wouldn't stop him.

He tucks my wind-blown hair behind an ear. "What is it about you, Ella?"

A cosmic force draws us together. We neither act on our attraction nor pull away, staring into each other's eyes, thinking and wondering, a silent probing. Even in my early days with Will, I never experienced anything like this.

Jack breaks the spell by picking up his camera. "Want to see my work?"

I'd rather kiss you. "Very much so."

After speeding through five photos, I touch his arm. "Please slow down. These are too special to rush."

"Didn't want to bore you."

"That will never happen."

Jack sees the ordinary and makes his subject unique with angles and lighting. I love how he captured the sun's reflection on the lighthouse. After showing me the last photo, I give him a well-deserved standing ovation.

"It's nice having a fan club." He chuckles. "I'm ready for lunch. How about you?"

"More pasta sounds good."

We retrace our steps and find a café near the harbor. Afterward, we stroll around, viewing art galleries and boutiques. We discover a watercolorist we both like although we differ on our favorite painting.

"Guess we'll have to buy both," he jokes.

We board the last ferry to the Cinque Terre. Jack puts his camera away for the ride home. We take in the views, my body tingling every time the boat tosses us together. I don't want this day to end.

TWENTY-NINE

O nce the boat leaves Monterosso, I get antsy. Vernazza is the next stop. It's now or never. "Thanks for inviting me to Portofino, Jack. I had a wonderful day. There's a restaurant in my village and, uh, I'm wondering if maybe you want—"

"To have dinner with you?"

Yes! "It's called Taverna Del Capitano."

"After the grueling work you did as my assistant, the least I can do is treat you to a meal." His serious expression turns into a warm smile. "How about I get cleaned up and meet you in front of the restaurant? Say seven-thirty?"

"Perfect! I'll make a reservation." My heart races, knowing our day won't end with the ferry ride.

When we arrive in Vernazza, Jack surprises me by getting off the boat. "Want to walk me to the train station?" He waves his pass. "Might as well make the most of it."

I nod, feeling my mouth stretch into a wide grin. *He wants to spend more time with me!*

I show him the stairs leading to my apartment. As we stroll through town, I point out my *panetteria*. I step inside and wave at Aberto. When we pass a gift shop, I gesture to a basket containing scented soaps. "Lavender and lemon are my favorites."

"You've settled quite nicely into Vernazza, haven't you?"

"That's the goal. My two weeks alone."

The last sentence slips out by accident. Jack looks pensive but doesn't press for an explanation. We arrive at the station as a train slows to a stop.

"It's been a pleasure spending the day with you, Ella. I'm looking forward to tonight." He steps on board. "And I'm glad you won't be dining alone."

I stare at the train long after it's gone. Never in my life have I had this type of connection with another person—except Tara. What is the universe telling me?

Back in the room, the shower is warm and refreshing. I swap out dry and wet clothes on the line, then relax in the chair, listening to music. Jack is such a gifted photographer. What an exciting life he must lead, traipsing around the world to capture its beauty. He's intelligent, kind, and focused. His touch sparks the type of electricity I've only dreamed about. Fate brought us together, not once but twice. That has to count for something, right?

I know he's attracted to me. He got off the ferry; we're having a second dinner. Am I ready for what might happen following a roman-tic evening of food, wine, and conversation? After all, we're only steps away from this apartment with no one looking over my shoulder.

Enough daydreaming. It's time to dig through my sparse wardrobe to find something to wear. Little black dress to the rescue. Off with the scarf. Too touristy. The silver necklace exudes elegance. Is the purse better over the shoulder or across the body? Shoulder, definitely.

I tidy up the room and lock the door. *You got this, Ella. Trust your instinct and don't be nervous. Enjoy yourself.*

THIRTY

The piazza's lights twinkle extra bright, and music plays to a lively crowd. Tempting aromas whet my appetite as I search for my dinner date. Seeing him standing by the restaurant makes my heart flutter. I hurry over.

"You look lovely, Ella." He kisses my cheek.

Umm... lavender soap. "Thanks."

A waiter escorts us to our table. Once we fumble through those first awkward minutes, we talk nonstop about Portofino over a bottle of wine and our meals. Jack feeds me bites of his seafood spaghetti; I share my walnut ravioli with him. We nibble on cannoli for dessert and sip chilled Limoncello, stretching out dinner for as long as possible.

After splitting the bill, we stroll around the piazza. Jack's fingers brush mine, and before long, he's holding my hand. Even though my insides are exploding like a Fourth of July extravaganza, I pretend it's no big deal. We end up at Santa Margherita d'Antiochia.

The ancient church has a spicy smell, similar to frankincense. There's also a musty odor as if water has seeped into its thick stone walls. Jack and I are near the altar browsing paintings and a wooden crucifix when he twists his neck from side to side. He's fidgety, unable to stand still.

"Are you okay?"

"Not really."

"What's going on?"

"Something I never expected." He rubs his neck. "Ella, I'm a thirty-eight-year-old man with lots of responsibilities. I came here to take photos, to get away. Then, we met. I can't stop thinking about you."

My chest tightens. He sounds almost angry as if meeting me was a bad thing, a disruption to his life.

"Why are you here by yourself?" he presses. "What's your story?"

My chest tightens even more. This is not a conversation I want to have. "I'm escaping, Jack. I have a lot going on at home."

"Don't we all?" Jack weaves his fingers through mine. "What I can't reconcile is my strong attraction to you after such a short time. Help me understand what's happening between us."

Stringing jumbled words together won't explain our connection. I must show him. I cup his face, kissing his forehead, making my way to his lips. Our tongues dance and swirl; neither of us holds back. He touches my hair, my back, all over. I press my body into him, our moans echoing in the church. Every sensation is new and wonderful, real and honest. Our passion is taking on a life of its own as my tears reach our mouths.

"You okay?" he says in between kisses. "Why are you crying?"

"They're happy tears, Jack. You make me feel things I didn't think were possible."

He nuzzles my neck. "I've been waiting for you, Ella. I didn't know it until yesterday on that trail. I want to tell you about my life, to learn everything about you."

My mouth goes dry. 'Everything' is such a far-reaching word. I sit on a wooden pew across from a marble sculpture of Jesus. The Son of God holds up a hand as if delivering a sermon on truth. Telling Jack my story means explaining why I took off my wedding ring, which leads to the rape. I don't want to go there. I want to replace those awful memories with new ones of him.

He is waiting for a response I don't want to give. Moments later, his shoulders slump. "We've had a long day, Ella. You're probably tired." He extends an arm. "Come, I'll walk you to your apartment."

I take his hand, not knowing what else to say or do. Indecision has paralyzed me. We make our way across the piazza, stopping at the bottom of my steps.

"I'm unsure what happened at the church," Jack says, "why you pulled away. I apologize if I came on too strong."

"You did nothing wrong."

He raises my chin until we're at eye level. "You bring out some powerful feelings in me. That scares me a little. I think it scares you, too."

Nothing about him, especially those lips and eyes, scares me. "I'm sorry I ruined our evening."

"You didn't ruin anything." He caresses my cheek. "May I see you tomorrow? Talk more after we're rested?"

He is so mature, pulling back but not away. Maybe I can tell him about Will, lay my cards on the table to see if we have a path forward. Tonight, I'll figure out the best way to explain my situation.

"I'd like that very much. Want to meet here for breakfast? Nine o'clock? Aberto makes tasty food."

"Sounds good." He kisses my forehead. "I look forward to seeing you in the morning. G'night, Ella."

He stuffs his hands in his pockets and strolls up Via Roma toward the train station. I drag my aching heart upstairs, wishing we'd never gone inside that stupid church.

THIRTY-ONE

A violent storm tosses my raft up one twelve-foot wave and down an-other. Wind slashes my face; rain pelts my body. I'm holding on for dear life as two men stand on a ship's bridge thirty yards away.

"Take my hand," one yells to me. "I'll save you!"

The other man shoves him. "Fuck off! She belongs to me!"

The men tumble to the deck, punching and clawing at each other. I'm paddling toward them to break up the fight; a rogue wave lobs me into the swirling sea. I'm sinking into a dark abyss, down, down, down...

I shoot up in bed, blinking my eyes awake. A dream. Another bad dream.

About Jack and Will.

And choices.

Starting a relationship with Jack before settling things with Will messes with my sense of order. Although I wish I'd met Jack later, fate brought us together now. He and I can't move forward until I come clean. About everything. No freaking out, no holding back, no filtering. Brutal honesty. If he's the man I believe he is, he'll accept me, warts and all. I'm sure he has one or two regrets. We are two imperfect people who might be perfect together. I want a chance to find out.

I splash water on my face, dress, and go downstairs. I'm surprised when Jack doesn't arrive by nine-fifteen. He's never late. By nine-thirty, I'm pacing. Does he think we're meeting at Aberto's shop? I jaunt over to have a look. Nothing. I return to the stairs, my stomach churning. Where is he? Why didn't we exchange phone numbers?

When ten o'clock rolls past—an hour after our scheduled meeting—I'm despondent. I can't sit idle any longer. I scamper to the station to check on the trains. They're running on schedule. Now what?

When one going to Riomaggiore stops, I climb aboard. I have no idea where Jack is staying. Who knows? I may get lucky since we have a habit of bumping into each other.

I hurry off the train. This village is bigger than Vernazza, row after row of identical-looking houses. Where do I begin?

Buzzing around town like a yellowjacket at a summer picnic produces no results. I knock on at least twenty hotel doors to see if he's a guest. Owners shake their heads when I can't produce Jack's last name. One man shoos me away as if I'm a groupie stalking a rock star. I show random people his picture. No one recognizes him.

I return to Vernazza, hoping to find him waiting by my steps. I'll describe my wild search; he'll share a similar story. We'll laugh about miscommunication and get on with our day.

He's not there.

A tear slips down my cheek. Why would he do this to me?

I hole up in my apartment, wondering what to do next. Jack and I shared something special; our connection was real. He held my hand; we kissed. He's the one who asked to meet today. He wanted to continue our conversation. Maybe he's in the piazza at this very moment. He'll never find me up here.

I rush downstairs and plant myself on a shaded bench with a water bottle. People stroll past, drawn to Vernazza like me. I keep an eye on the restaurant where Jack and I ate last night. I peek inside the church a few times. He's not at either place. I visit the train station and look inside the shops. He's nowhere to be found.

I circle back to my stairs, sitting through the sunset, twilight, and dusk. As the piazza's lights fade and the music stops, I lumber upstairs to my apartment. I came to Vernazza to be alone. My wish has come true in a way I never imagined.

My body feels sluggish the next morning as if I'm swimming in watery mud. Jack is gone and isn't returning. I must accept this depressing fact. A dove lands on my windowsill, cooing. Another one joins him, then a third. They're pecking at the breadcrumbs I put there yesterday. Tara released doves at Mom's funeral to ease my sorrow. Have they flown here to taunt me?

I press a cold cloth on my swollen eyes. I can either continue to mope or get on with living. I came to Vernazza for many reasons; Jack the photographer wasn't one of them. I cry one last time, then vow to never shed another tear over a man I barely knew.

THIRTY-TWO

A routine of hiking, eating, and exploring the region emerges. Besides Cinque Terre's five villages, I visit Levanto, Bonassola, and Santa Margherita Ligure. For a couple of mornings, I linger in Vernazza to soak up the town's charm.

Every day without fail, two brothers, Arturo and Paolo, meet for breakfast. The years have carved lines into their faces. They sip their coffee slowly, having retired their watches long ago. I insert myself into their conversations and get the inside scoop about Vernazza's history, their families, and the daily fishing report.

"Our village only one with a port," Arturo says proudly. "We fight pirates. We also have bad times."

He goes on to describe a devastating flood that occurred in the Cinque Terre on October 25, 2011, where thirteen people died. Vernazza was destroyed and had to be rebuilt. Hiking trails remained inaccessible for more than a year.

"We okay," Paolo says, "but flood chase away my family." He pulls out a picture from his wallet. "This is Lorenzo, my grandson. He famous guide, speak five languages. Too bad he move to Milan. You make nice couple, Ella."

Lorenzo reminds me of the waiter I met on my first night with his wavy hair, almond complexion, and engaging smile. I'm tempted to visit Milan and book a private tour.

This is my last evening in the Cinque Terre. No more fantasy days in Italy. I've stretched a ten-day vacation into a month-long adventure without an ounce of regret. I'm comfortable traveling anywhere at a moment's notice; strangers are one conversation away from becoming friends.

For dinner, I'm torturing myself by eating at the restaurant in Manarola where Jack shared his table with me. I thought the universe had long-term plans for us. Instead, all we had was an incredible two-day fling.

I've met dozens of people in Italy, and no one affected me like the enigmatic photographer. I hardly knew him, yet he opened my eyes as to what I want in my next relationship: passion, respect, wit, laughter, spontaneity, and kindness.

Maybe he's one of those earth angels who wanders around saving troubled souls, staying only long enough to mend broken hearts before moving on. I touch my lips, remembering our kiss. The sensations inside of me have nothing to do with celestial beings.

One day I'll find my person. Until then, I raise a glass to Jack without any bitterness. "Thank you for showing me a better way to live."

Today is August 2, the day I leave my beloved village. I rise early and stroll to the harbor, soaking in the burnt-orange sun rising above the sea. Vernazza has embraced me with hospitality, generosity, and truth. I will miss her.

Aberto has breakfast ready when I enter his shop. He knows it's my last day and won't let me pay. I sit with Arturo and Paolo on our bench, passing over two pastries. They've added new English words to their vocabulary, and I've learned useful Italian phrases.

My last walk on Via Roma is a slow one as I sear in memories. Staying in Vernazza was the right decision. My time here taught me that destiny is more of a journey rather than an endpoint. If I look forward to each sunrise, if my days are joyous, fulfilling, and meaningful, if I give to others, then I'm living my destiny. I will never forget this enchanting village for as long as I live.

A train returns me to Florence where I drop off my bags at a hotel and hop on a bus to the city center. I stroll past the Duomo, Uffizi Gallery, and the Ponte Vecchio Bridge one last time, and eat dinner at an outside café, comfortable with my aloneness.

When I was young, my dad set up a table for jigsaw puzzles in our family room. Occasionally, we'd finish one in a day. Other times, we'd fit in pieces here and there, taking weeks to complete it. Either way, we ended up with a picture hanging in our garage.

I arrived in Italy a month ago toting a poorly-assembled puzzle of my life. I'm leaving with its new edges firmly in place, the pieces rearranged into meaningful chunks. Now, it's time to return home and finish the work.

THIRTY-THREE

After a grueling travel day, I land at SFO in the late afternoon, retrieve my luggage, and clear customs. Tara is jumping up and down in the visitor section, waving her arms.

"You're back!" We twirl around, becoming a human merry-go-round. "You look fabulous! I love the tan, your hat, the skirt. You've turned into an Italian!"

Tara takes one of my suitcases, and we walk to the parking garage. She lowers her MINI Cooper's top, taking advantage of the warm August weather. We break free of the airport chaos and maneuver through snarled traffic, each mile returning me to unfinished business. Twenty-four hours earlier, I was eating gelato in Florence. Now, I'm on a crowded freeway on my way to uncertainty.

"I stocked your fridge with essentials and picked up your mail as a welcome home gift." Tara taps her finger on the steering wheel. "Ready for a William Walker update?"

"Not really."

"Ready or not, here it comes." She shifts positions. "I called him when I got back. He went ballistic, became a raving lunatic."

"What'd you tell him?"

"The truth. That I found a great last-minute travel deal for your birthday. I stayed cryptic so I didn't set him off."

"His reaction?"

"I think his exact words were *No fucking way she does anything without my permission.* He called me a homewrecker, said to mind my own g-d business. He's pissed I left you alone in Italy. He assumed you were shacking up with a lover."

I sink into the headrest and close my eyes. "Does he know I'm home?"

"He knows you're arriving this week but not when."

I slide a mint in my mouth and pass one to Tara. "I'm divorcing him and moving to Piedmont. Our marriage is over."

Tara sucks on the mint instead of responding. I thought she'd be thrilled to learn I finally made a decision. Instead, she's pensive, almost detached. She probably doesn't believe I'll follow through. I'll have to show her.

THIRTY-FOUR

I set my luggage in the living room. Piedmont isn't Vernazza but it's home. I flip on a ceiling fan and open windows to get air circulating. "Thanks for moving my car from your flat."

"Thank Dylan. He drove." Tara snickers. "Younger brothers are occasionally useful. I'll pour wine and meet you out back."

The shaded patio feels nice compared to the stuffy house. Roses and gladiolus are in full bloom, pansies and impatiens have been added to the mix by my skilled gardener. Tara joins me on the swing and passes over a glass.

"So, you're divorcing the evil one and moving here?"

"That's the plan. I also resigned from my job."

Tara chokes on her wine, spraying it on the cement. *"You what?"*

I set my glass down. "You are impossible to read today, Tara Collins. You had an odd reaction in the car after I told you about the divorce. Now you seem…I don't know…unimpressed with my plans to move forward. What's going on?"

She crosses her leg, wiggling her foot as if it's on fire. "Will isn't letting you go without a fight. Things will get messy. And working at the hospital gave you purpose. Those babies grounded you."

"Are you worried I'm moving too fast?"

"Only with your job. Not Will. The sooner you get rid of him the better. But the divorce will turn his life upside down. Who knows what he'll do?" Tara shifts in her chair. "You must hire a savvy lawyer, Ella. Neither my team nor I can represent you. Any connection to me is poison. I have referrals for you."

"Thanks, but I already have someone in mind. As for work, I want to leave my comfort zone, try something new. Italy taught me how to do that." I try suppressing a yawn but it escapes anyway.

"I'm losing you to jet lag, aren't I?"

"Yeah, I'm exhausted."

Tara finishes her wine and stands. "Promise me you won't be alone with Will. Keep your interactions over the phone. When the two of you talk, have a purpose. Don't give him wiggle room or he'll make your life miserable. He'll try to erode your confidence and say or do anything—"

I clasp Tara's hand to stop her rant. "I appreciate your wise words, the lift home, and the food. You know it's because of you I'm able to make these changes, right?"

"And that's my cue to hit the road."

"Please know I heard what you said. We'll talk again in a few days."

I walk Tara to the front door and wave as she drives off. Will sure has her wound her up. He'll try and do the same to me except his tactics won't work. I'll let him vent. After all, I did abandon him for a month. We won't wallow in misery, though. He and I will move toward an amicable divorce. Why make ending an unhealthy marriage contentious? More than anything, I want my freedom.

A stack of mail and my overstuffed suitcases are begging for attention. They'll have to wait. I'm too tired to unpack, sort, eat, read, or think. It's four in the morning in Florence and seven at night in Piedmont. A bath and a good night's sleep will hopefully acclimate me.

I climb into the tub, turn on the hot water, and sprinkle lavender bath salts. *Ahh...* Pure luxury after a month of showers. I slide down to my neck and close my eyes. Instead of Tara's worried face, I see streaks of pink, orange, and purple flash across the Italian sky. I see sunflowers, castles, walled cities, pastel houses, hiking trails, ancient farmhouses, and villages. I see happy couples, friends, and families treating one another with respect, kindness, and love. I see a bright future waiting for me.

I just have to get past William Walker first.

THIRTY-FIVE

I wake up groggy the next morning, forcing myself from bed. Crossing time zones sure messes with the body's internal clock.

I call my lawyer and schedule a late-afternoon appointment, then shuffle to the kitchen. The cinnamon-raisin bagels, peanut butter, and tea bags on the counter make me smile. I find eggs, orange juice, strawberries, grapes, and three pre-made salads inside the refrigerator. Tara knows exactly what I like.

Living alone has spoiled me. If I use a dish, I wash it. Clothes go in the hamper. No TV droning in the background. I sort the mail and throw away most of it, browsing a Homes and Gardens magazine while munching on a bagel.

Time for laundry. Yay! I have a washer and dryer. I'll never take that duo for granted again. A salty odor seeps out after opening my suitcases, reminding me of Vernazza. I remove a shirt from the pile and seal it in a Ziplock bag to preserve its scent.

Decision time. Do I continue sleeping in my old room or move to Mom's? Her bedroom is larger and has an adjoining bath. She'd never approve of a shrine. I force myself to empty her drawers and closet, putting items in bags destined for the homeless shelter. That will make her happy.

An alarm rings, reminding me it's time to meet with my attorney. Driving a car is nerve-racking after a month of using public transportation. People race past as if gaining an extra minute makes a difference.

A secretary escorts me to Mr. Abram's office.

"Hello, Ella. It's good to see you." He gestures to an empty chair. "Is your husband joining us?"

"No. It's just me. I read the trust and want to continue our conversation. I also want to learn how to access money."

"Very good. Your mom appointed me the trustee of her estate. The trust pays me a fee to fulfill that role. Once we settle the charitable donation, you inherit the rest of the assets. Do you have any questions about these facts?"

"No. I'm clear."

"Two matters require attention: filing a final IRS return on Margaret's behalf and having the Piedmont property assessed for tax purposes. Shall I proceed with both items?"

"Yes, please."

"I partner with a wealth manager, Peter Murphy, to handle your investments. Here's the latest financial report." Mr. Abrams passes over a folder. "Your mother invested 40% in stocks, 50% in bonds, and 10% in cash. Pete wants you to complete a risk questionnaire so he can tailor the portfolio to meet your goals."

"I'm fine with what Mom set up."

"Okay. I'll let him know." He glances at his notes. "You asked about accessing money. The trust transfers three thousand dollars each month into your checking account. If you want to adjust the amount—up or down—let me know. You'll find a checkbook and debit card with your name in the folder."

"Thanks for answering my financial questions. May I switch topics?"

"Certainly. What's on your mind?"

"My husband isn't here today because I'm divorcing him. I was hoping you'd handle the paperwork."

Mr. Abrams sits back in his chair, rocking. "Family law isn't my specialty. I have a colleague who will represent you." He culls through a desk drawer and hands me a business card. "Jim is *very* skilled at his job."

I tuck the card in my purse, suppressing a smile. He doesn't even try to hide his delight over my marriage's demise. "I'm aware Will isn't legally entitled to my inheritance. May I use trust money to pay off mutual debt?"

Mr. Abrams purses his lips. "It's your money, Ella. I caution you not to put the cart before the horse. Let Jim handle those details."

Better leave while I'm ahead. "Thanks for squeezing me in today. I won't take any more of your time."

A weight lifts from my shoulders as I leave his office knowing my finances are in order. The first check goes to Tara to reimburse her for my travel expenses. I'm also giving her a painting so she never forgets the effect that she—and Vernazza—had on my life.

That evening, I ponder how to approach Will. What I have to say can't be done via phone. I refuse to be alone with him and don't want Tara involved. She's done enough to help me. Meeting him at a crowded restaurant seems like the safest bet. It's neutral territory that allows for an easy retreat. My hands tremble as I make the call.

"Well, if it isn't my devoted wife."

"Hello, Will. I guess we have a lot to talk about."

"That's putting it mildly. Where are you?"

"In Piedmont. Please don't come over. I have jet lag. Are you available for dinner on Friday at The Spinnaker?"

"Too noisy. Let's meet at home."

I stay focused, knowing what would happen if we were alone in Mill Valley. "I prefer a restaurant. Friday? Six-thirty?"

He says nothing.

Neither do I. He can't touch me over the phone.

"Fine." He waits for a beat then adds, "I missed you, Ella. I'm looking forward to seeing you."

After ending the call, I'm struck by the tension in my body and the frostiness in his voice. This reunion will not be pleasant.

THIRTY-SIX

I arrive early at the restaurant to stake out the place. When the hostess leads me to a table with a water view, I gesture to the back wall, a place no one wants to sit.

"Um, we have all of these tables." She shows me three coveted dining spots.

"Near the kitchen will be fine."

She shrugs and lays menus down. "Let me know if you change your mind."

She'll learn why I chose this area soon enough. I move the menus against the wall to get them out of the way. Workers rush in and out of the kitchen, carrying plates. Pots and pans are clanging as I rearrange the condiments on the table. The front door opens. It's him. *Breathe.*

Will arrives decked out in a dark blue suit and open-collared white shirt. Driving a convertible keeps him tanned, and exercising at the gym maintains his muscular physique. Two women at the bar ogle him as he searches the room. I used to look at him that way. Not anymore.

Our eyes lock. He strides over, holding up both palms. "Why are you sitting over here?"

And so the drama begins. "Thanks for coming." I gesture at the seat across from me.

He scowls, running a hand through his hair. Then, like sunlight breaking through thick clouds, his trademark smile emerges, the one he uses to charm clients.

"Where we sit isn't important." Will kisses my cheek. "You look lovely, Ella. Italy agrees with you. You'll have to take me there one day so we can enjoy it together."

"I had an incredible time. Tara knew exactly what I needed."

The smile dissipates. "I'm your husband. You didn't give me a chance to—"

A server arrives, setting bread and a shallow bowl of vinegar and oil on the table. "Good evening. What would you like to drink?"

I jump to answer so Will doesn't explode over the interruption. "I'll have a Pellegrino with lemon, please."

"And for you, sir?"

"Draft beer, house special. Cold mug." Will shoos away the server. "So, Ella. Why are you staying at Margaret's instead of coming home?" His eyes are intense, probing.

Be direct, don't ramble. "I feel safer living apart from you."

"What's that supposed to mean?"

"We both know our marriage isn't working. We've been drifting apart for months. After the shower incident—"

"Don't start with that bullshit."

I briefly close my eyes. "And that's why we're in trouble, Will. You never listen to me. You dismiss what I say."

"And *you* ran away for a month while I paid *our* bills. You might want to lose the holier-than-thou attitude."

Don't let him intimidate you. "I have things to tell you. Do you want to listen or should I leave?"

He sits back and folds his arms, motioning for me to continue.

Okay. Deep breath. "You dominate me in a way I find oppressive. We rarely enjoy each other's company. We're roommates, not partners. I want kids, you don't. We're out of sync on so many levels." I mix the balsamic vinegar and olive oil together. "We're like this duo, unable to blend as one." I set the spoon down, watching the amber and black liquids retreat from each other.

He presses bread into the liquid until it's saturated with both ingredients and delivers a victory smile, mocking me.

"Forcing things to work is exhausting, Will. I want more—"

The server returns with our drinks. "Are you ready to order?"

"Go away," Will growls, pushing his glass aside. "Can't you see we're in the middle of something?"

Will refocuses on me. "You were saying?"

"We're not good for each other; we want different things and have competing priorities. I think it's best if we part ways."

He clenches his jaw. "That's never happening."

"I have a right to express—"

"You lost whatever rights you had after you lied about that bullshit party and took off." He leans across the table. "Look, I haven't asked what you did in Italy or who you did it with. Be grateful. I don't care if..."

My body trembles as he ups the verbal attack. People are staring, whispering. I'm shrinking smaller, losing confidence, and ready to run when the most unexpected image appears in my mind. Jack is holding my hand on the ferry in Portofino to protect me from the crowd. I feel his warmth, his caring, his kindness. The memory reminds me of what I want in a partner, and it's not the bully sitting across from me.

"Stop talking! Now!"

He freezes mid-sentence.

"I need you to listen, Will. Our marriage is over. I'm filing for divorce."

He tosses up both hands. "What in the hell am I supposed to do, Ella? We have a mortgage, car payments, credit cards. You're leaving me high and dry."

It's always about him. "Don't worry. I'll make sure you're financially stable."

He flops back in his chair. "So, you'll help with the bills?"

The only connection between us is anger and desperation. I said what I came to say; it's time to go. I place money on the table and stand.

"You're leaving?"

If I stay, it's only a matter of time until he overpowers me. I won't let that happen. "We'll call and text but I don't want to see you anymore. I'm sorry, Will."

"You're sorry? You fuck me over and you're sorry? You're making a huge mistake, Ella. I'm the one who married damaged goods. I'm the best thing that's ever happened to you!"

Every minute I spend with this man, I lose a piece of my soul. His ruthless behavior tells me I'm making the right decision to end the marriage. I walk outside; he follows. I open my car door. "I get that you're angry, Will. Deep down, you know we're better off apart."

"Don't tell me what I know!" He lowers his voice as a security guard watches us from across the parking lot. "You've changed, Ella. What happened in Italy?"

"I discovered what's important."

"And it's not me?"

"You have our savings to use while we sort this out."

"Does this mean you're not selling Piedmont as we agreed?"

My blood boils. *"We* never agreed to sell anything! That was your fantasy, not mine."

He cracks his knuckles. "You'll take my calls?"

"Of course. I want us both to be happy. It's—"

"You wouldn't know happy if it bit you in the ass."

He flings more insults, calling me a lazy bitch for not working.

I screech out of the parking lot and drive straight home. Even though the confrontation rattles me, I'm relieved it's over. I lock the doors and windows, activate the alarm, and pray he leaves me alone.

THIRTY-SEVEN

Tara and I meet in Berkeley on Saturday for breakfast where I tell her about the restaurant incident.

"I wish you'd recorded Will's threats," she says. "I could've gotten a restraining order."

"I didn't sleep much. He really scared me."

"Stay away from him, Ella. No more face-to-face meetings. And keep the alarm on, even during the day."

She doesn't have to twist my arm.

After a short hike in Tilden Regional Park, we return to my house where a wrapped package is waiting on a table.

"For me?" Tara asks with genuine surprise.

"Open the card first."

She reads my note and waves the check. "Way too much."

"Not for what you did for me. Open the gift."

She rips off the paper, smiling. "Vernazza?"

"Home, sweet, home."

The watercolor triggers many stories; she listens to each one. I point out the stairs to my apartment, the bench by the harbor, the church, the *panetteria,* and *gelateria.*

Tara leaves to attend her sister's birthday party. She invited me to go, but Will has bombarded me with texts and calls. I want time alone to ponder my next steps.

On Monday, I call my supervisor at the hospital. Returning to my comfort zone doesn't feel like moving forward. I'm ready to try something different. Even though I emailed my resignation from Italy, I speak with Anne about my decision. Mom taught me never to burn bridges.

I visit the Mill Valley house in the late morning to pick up my belongings. I didn't call first, trying to avoid a confrontation. That was a big mistake.

"Open the goddamn door!" Will screams that evening from my front porch.

"Go away," I say from inside the locked house.

"I wouldn't be here if you didn't trespass, you conniving bitch!"

"Excuse me," my neighbor yells from her porch. "Is there a problem?" Susan holds up a phone. "The police are on speed dial."

Will runs his hands through his hair. He kicks the door, introduces Susan to his middle finger, and speeds away. I wave to her through a window, mouthing a grateful *thank you.* Our neighborhood watch leader returns a reassuring thumbs-up.

The following day, I meet with the attorney to initiate divorce proceedings. Once Will learns I'm paying off the Mill Valley mortgage and transferring the deed to him, he miraculously stops calling and texting.

Who says money can't buy happiness?

THIRTY-EIGHT

Over the next several weeks, I clean out more closets, drawers, and cabinets, giving unwanted items to charity. I paint the master bedroom celestial blue, a color that lives up to its name. I buy a firmer mattress for Mom's antique bed. A new comforter and down-feather pillows make the room mine.

With the house in order and my divorce proceeding, it's time to focus on my career. A job search uncovers two exciting possibilities. One is travel nursing. I'd work through an agency on short-term gigs around the country. I decide when and where, and for how long. The position offers lots of freedom at a premium salary, allowing me to visit different parts of the United States.

A second option is working for an organization called Doctors Without Borders. According to their website, they provide medical assistance to disaster victims throughout the world, a job that speaks to my heart. I email my resume to see if they bite.

I also look into adopting a child. The process is daunting with a background check, a home study, and many decisions to make: baby or older child? Gender? Born in the U.S. or another country? The questions are endless. Between the divorce and my job situation, the timing is off. I put adoption on the back burner until my life settles down.

Today I'm learning how to make a digital photo album. Pictures of Montecatini, the spa, Florence, San Gimignano, Cinque Terre, and others are too good not to immortalize. The one of Tara and me standing in that whale's mouth gets a whole page if I figure out how to—

Ringgg!

I don't recognize the number. "Hello?"

"Ella?"

"Yes. Who's calling?"

"My name is Jenna McQuinn. Will and I work together."

"What's going on, Jenna?"

"We're in Colorado on a business trip. Will got a really bad headache and slurred his words."

"Is he all right?"

"No, he's not," Jenna cries. "The paramedics rushed him to the hospital. He has a tumor, Ella. In his brain. The doctor wants to do surgery and Will is freaking out."

My stomach drops as if I'm racing up an express elevator in San Francisco's tallest building.

"He wants you here to explain stuff."

She can't be serious.

"What should I tell him?"

If what she's saying is true, this is horrible news. I feel awful for him but he is no longer my responsibility. "Put him on the phone, Jenna."

"He, uh… Will's scared you won't come if he asks. I'm begging you, Ella. Set aside your differences and do this for him! *All* of us need to support him! *Please!*"

The desperation in her voice makes me hyperventilate. Jenna McQuinn has boxed me in a corner, or rather Will has since he orchestrated the call. He expects me to drop everything and come running as usual.

"Ella?"

I hunch over, rubbing my temples. I'm damned if I go and damned if I stay. He's treated me so awful, yet how can I live with myself if I abandon him at a time like this? He has no one else. And legally, I'm still his wife.

My stomach tightens. "Let him know I'll be there tomorrow. I'll text the details." I reluctantly book a flight that lands in Denver close to eleven. I call Tara to share the unfortunate news.

"Ella, I'm sorry about his health, but don't forget he put you through the wringer. You can't let him suck you in again."

He already has. I end the call with a heavy heart. No matter what legal steps I take, no matter how much time passes, I'll always be tethered to William Walker one way or another because we said vows.

I guess money doesn't buy happiness after all.

THIRTY-NINE

I land in Denver and set the rental car's GPS for Boulder Community Hospital. After passing a mall called Flatiron Crossing on I-36, the landscape bursts with openness and flora. I can't stop staring at the Rockies. If I become a travel nurse, I'm listing Colorado as a preferred destination. This place is gorgeous.

I'm sure Will isn't enjoying the views. It's hard to imagine him lying in a hospital bed. He hates depending on others, always wanting to do things for himself. Is his tumor benign like a meningioma? Malignant like a glioblastoma? Is the surgery urgent or can it wait? Is it complex or straightforward? What about ongoing care? There are too many questions and not enough answers.

I arrive at the hospital, taking a moment to center myself. Will needs me to be calm, not anxious. A friendly volunteer directs me to his room where I find two men slumped in chairs watching television. A woman who is sitting on his bed jumps up as our eyes meet, pink creeping across her cheeks.

"Hello, Ella." She extends a hand. "I'm Jenna. Thanks for coming."

She's an attractive, athletic-looking woman who is comfortable speaking on Will's behalf. I've seen her and the men at the airport during pick-up runs but we've never spoken.

"Hi, there." Will scoots up in bed, looking at his team. "Guys? Give us a minute, okay?"

"We'll be right outside." Jenna motions for the men to follow her.

Will turns off the TV. "It's good to see you, Ella." He speaks in a subdued voice, his cockiness gone. "I know you didn't have to come."

"Jenna didn't give me much choice." I pull up a chair. "Tell me what's going on."

He cracks his knuckles. "I have this thing in my head. The doctor wants to cut it out. He's scaring the hell out of me."

"Does this 'thing' have a name?"

"It's mumbo-jumbo to me. That's why I needed you." He glances out the window, his eyes welling with tears. "You'll give it to me straight."

I've never seen him behave this way. He usually pushes through challenges with bravado. Not today. He's terrified and who can blame him?

Will picks up a folder from a side table. "Here's what the white coat gave me."

After seeing a neurosurgeon's name and a meningioma information sheet, I realize he isn't exaggerating.

"Can you talk to him?" Will begs. "Sort this out? Help me decide what to do? This is my brain we're talking about."

I give his hand a reassuring squeeze. "That's why I'm here."

"I knew you'd come through for me, Ella. You always do."

For the first time in months, I see real sincerity in his eyes and hear humility in his voice. This health scare has forced him to grow up overnight. Perhaps there's hope for him after all.

I drive a short distance to a modern, two-story stone building with dark windows. Neurosurgery signs direct me to the second floor.

"May I help you?" a perky receptionist says.

"Yes, good afternoon. I'm Ella Walker. My husband, William Walker, was admitted to the hospital by Doctor Thornton. I'd like to speak with him, please."

"Oh, I'm sorry, Mrs. Walker. He's booked all afternoon. May I have him call you later?"

"No, I want to talk in person. I'll wait."

A staring contest results in her blinking first. "I'll see what I can arrange. Please take a seat."

I thumb through magazines as people come and go. Forty-five minutes later, the receptionist guides me to a large corner office.

"Doctor Thornton will be with you shortly." She closes the door.

I'm immediately drawn to a window that overlooks the mountain range. The colors and layers are spectacular. Another wall is covered with framed diplomas from Dartmouth College and Harvard Medical School, along with certificates for a residency at Johns Hopkins and a fellowship in skull base surgery from Cornell. Will lucked out. This doctor has impressive credentials.

On the desk is a framed photograph of a boy and girl. Cute kids. Another photo of a man, a boy, and a pregnant woman catches my eye. I hold the frame closer. Blood drains from my face.

No way. Not possible. Things like this don't happen.

The door opens.

I look into those sapphire eyes that captured my heart in Italy. Jack steps back. *"Ella?"*

I'm frozen, unable to talk or move.

He closes the door and takes the frame from my hand, returning it to his desk. "What's going on? I was expecting the wife of a patient."

I close my eyes, barely able to comprehend what's unfolding in this room. "Nice to meet you, Doctor Thornton. I'm Mrs. Walker."

Jack's posture stiffens. He doesn't know what to say or do, either. It's as if we're middle-schoolers at our first dance, awkward and uncomfortable waiting for the other one to make the first move.

"Let's start over." He loosens his tie. "Your husband needs surgery; you have questions. Is this why you're here?"

"Yes, that's true." I gesture at a photograph. "How old are your children, Jack?"

He tilts his head as he did in Italy. "Lucas is six. Rose turned three in June."

"Rose looks like you. Lucas resembles his mother."

He rubs his neck. "Ella, you didn't come here to talk about my family. What questions do you have about your *husband*?"

His accusatory tone galls me. What a hypocrite.

"Will said you want to operate yet doesn't understand his condition. I flew from California to support him. That's why I'm here."

Jack nods, giving little else away. He launches into an explanation of Will's condition but I can't concentrate. Why did he pursue me in Italy when he has this beautiful family? Why lead me to believe he was a professional photographer? No wonder he left town so abruptly. Everything about him was a lie.

"Ella?" Jack sighs. "Have you heard anything I've said? You seem distracted."

That's an understatement. "You're right, and I apologize. You have my full attention." *The faster we talk, the faster I'm out of here.*

"Are you really a nurse?"

"What's that supposed to mean?"

"I'll provide technical details if you are. Otherwise, I'll speak in layman's terms."

Once again, I don't appreciate his tone. "Yes, I'm a registered nurse." I remove a notepad and pen from my purse. "Don't omit anything."

Jack briefly closes his eyes. "Will was admitted with severe headaches, dizziness, and slurred speech. An MRI revealed a convexity meningioma growing over the left hemisphere. There's significant edema. He requires surgery to release the pressure so it doesn't damage the brain. Questions?"

"How long has he had the tumor?"

"It's hard to tell. Months or even years."

"Would it make him act in unusual ways such as loud, demanding, hyperactive?"

"No. It's the headaches, dizziness, and other physical symptoms that define the problem."

"Okay. Please continue."

"The tumor can be removed intact by placing gentle traction on the dural attachment and working circumferentially around it to relieve pressure on the cortex. If I can't visualize the tumor's surface, I may attempt an internal decompression. Does this make sense to you?"

I nod even though I don't understand everything he says. I get the gist of it.

He watches me closely. "Most tumors are removed with little or no damage to the brain while others are difficult to extract. I won't know until I go in. Your husband may have partial paralysis, changes in sensation, weakness, or poor thinking."

Thoughts of Will requiring long-term care give me acid indigestion. "Do you anticipate these problems given his symptoms and MRI findings?"

"No. I believe it'll be a straightforward extraction." Jack shifts his weight. "The tumor is causing problems and must come out. Would you like a second opinion? Prefer another neurosurgeon to operate?"

He's giving me an out. I should take it after what happened in Italy. But this isn't about me. It's about Will's health. Jack's passion for medicine is on par with photography. My intuition and those diplomas on the wall tell me Will is in capable hands.

"That's unnecessary. If Will agrees to have surgery, when can you operate?"

He pulls out his phone and studies a calendar. "The day after tomorrow, early afternoon."

"I'll talk with Will and let you know."

"If you want, I'll swing by the hospital later. He was agitated this morning. Might help if the three of us discuss this together."

"Good idea. What time?"

"Between five-thirty and six."

We gaze at each other, our connection still palpable despite those pictures on his desk. I flee from his office, praying for a new kind of strength.

FORTY

I stop at Peet's on my way to the hospital. Nothing calms me like a mixture of ginger, cinnamon, cloves, black pepper, and cardamom. And boy, do I need calming.

I sink into a comfy chair with my chai. There are thousands of hospitals in America. Why did Will have to get sick in Boulder, Colorado?

I can't believe Jack is married. With two adorable kids. Thornton. Jack Thornton. Doctor Jack Thornton. At least he wasn't a hallucination.

A woman sporting yoga clothes walks into the coffee shop. Her coiffed blonde hair and tawny-colored eyes make her a dead ringer for Jack's wife. Who takes care of the kids while she's out maintaining a size-two figure? Naturally, she orders a skinny latte.

Why am I still attracted to him knowing he has a family? He seemed genuine, the real deal. His words circle in my mind: *I can't stop thinking about you; help me understand our attraction.* I fell for the scam hook, line, and sinker.

I scroll through my travel photos until I reach Jack's picture, my finger hovering over the delete button. *"Press it!"* my subconscious demands. *"Now!"*

I can't do it. I can't erase him. I want to remember how he made me feel.

Talk about hypocrites.

I took off my wedding ring. I flirted with Jack knowing I was married. I initiated the kissing, hoping for more. It's time to pay for those indiscretions.

Will is about to undergo a major operation. Healing from this type of surgery takes weeks—and that's if all goes well. He'll need someone to look after him. I toss my empty cup into the garbage and set course for the hospital to begin my penance.

I glance through a window as I approach Will's room. He's alone with Jenna who is holding a cup as he drinks through a straw. She laughs, hanging onto his every word. *Don't they look cozy?*

I push open the door; Jenna hops off the bed, blushing. Will scoots up. "That was quick. What'd the white coat have to say?"

I tip my head at Jenna. Will takes my cue and asks her to leave. Once we're alone, I explain the tumor and encourage him to have the operation.

"What if I do nothing?"

"The swelling will make your symptoms worse and may lead to bleeding in your brain."

"The guy isn't a quack? You trust him?"

"Doctor Thornton is more than qualified. He's stopping by later to talk with us."

He cracks his knuckles. "Can surgery wait until I get home? You must know a bigwig at your hospital."

"Waiting is risky because of the swelling. Your headache and dizziness may get worse. Also, you don't want something to go wrong at thirty-thousand feet. If you want a different surgeon, I'll find one."

Will stares out the window, lost in thought.

I pat his leg. "You have a big decision to make. I'll check in at the hotel to give you time to think."

"I want you here when that doctor returns."

"I'll be back within an hour."

He cracks his knuckles again. "Send Jenna in, okay? She needs to know the plan to keep everyone informed."

I glance through the window on my way out. Jenna approaches Will with a tender smile; he gives her a playful grin. She says something, tapping his nose. Oh, they're definitely a couple. Why am I here if he has her? What game is he playing?

FORTY-ONE

I register at the hotel, call and update Tara, then return to the hospital. Will and I continue discussing his condition. After a robust debate, he decides to move forward with the surgery.

He is sleeping and I'm reading a novel when Jack steps into the room. I set my book aside, my body tingling in the wrong places. He's handsome in his coat, shirt, and tie. Picturing him wearing khakis and hiking boots makes reconciling the real man difficult.

He motions for me to join him. "Hello, Ella. Has Will made a decision?"

"He's ready to sign the consent."

Jack looks relieved. "Does he have questions?"

"I'm sure—"

Will wakes up. "Hey, doc. Back to see your favorite patient?"

"I was telling Doctor Thornton you want to move forward with surgery. He asked if—"

Jenna and the guys stop at the door. "Um, looks like you're busy. Want us to come back?"

"Nah, stay." Will waves them in. "The more, the merrier. Ella, get some chairs. And have my nurse—the cute redhead—bring us something to eat. Hell, have her order pizzas for everyone."

His friends pile into the room, hooting and hollering as if they're at a frat party. My stomach churns when Will laughs with them, his humbleness gone. His usual swagger is on full display.

"Will?" I say patiently. "Perhaps it's best if we talk to Doctor Thornton in private."

He glances at Jack, looks at his team, then lands on me. I cringe, having seen that expression many times. He's about to push limits.

"Not necessary. These clowns know everything about me."

Jack clears his throat. "Do you have questions about the procedure, Will?"

"Nope. My soon-to-be-ex broke it down." He winks at his buddies. "She's good at that."

They laugh at my expense, humiliating me. I cast an evil eye at Will. If he doesn't turn this around, I'm driving to the airport tonight.

His grin melts like butter in a hot skillet. "Ella explained what's going on, Doc. She says you know what you're doing. Go for it."

Jack glances at me before saying, "Okay. I'll start the paperwork."

Will smirks at his friends. "But I better enjoy myself in case you remove my brain by accident." He and his buddies roar with laughter.

"Don't be so dramatic," Jenna says.

Or be so predictable, I silently add.

One of the guys tosses him a jumbo Hershey Bar. "Here's sugar medicine to heal you. We can't lose our deal-closer."

More laughter.

Jack and I step into the hallway, retreating from the circus. He chortles. "You certainly have your hands full."

"You have no idea." I rub my chest to soothe the tightness.

He tips his head at Will's room. "After witnessing that mania, I do."

"Well, I did warn you in Italy I was escaping. Now, you know from whom."

He tosses me a sideways glance but says nothing.

"Get ready," I warn him as we stroll down the corridor. "Will can be challenging. You're only seeing the tip of the iceberg."

"Don't worry. I'll handle him." He clears his throat. "How long have you been married?"

"Six years."

"Do you have kids?"

"No." *And where's this going?*

"Are you really divorcing?"

My jaw drops. *He's so out of line!*

His phone chirps; he glances at it. "You remain a mystery for me, Ella. One day I'll solve it. Right now, I'm needed in the ER. We'll talk again tomorrow." He presses a button, begins talking, and walks away, leaving me with my mouth hanging open.

Who does he think he is asking such personal questions? Between Jack's arrogance and Will's immaturity, this is going to be a challenging week.

FORTY-TWO

Well, it's happening. My soon-to-be-ex is in the operating room having a tumor removed by my former travel buddy. Wouldn't that make a catchy headline for the six o'clock news?

Will put Jenna in charge of their division during his absence and sent the three of them home yesterday. Getting him through this medical odyssey has officially fallen on me.

After sitting for hours, I pace in the waiting room. Is the surgery going well? Any surprises? Should I call Will's mom to let her know what's happening? Probably not. It's best to stay out of his business.

I finish my novel and read every magazine in the waiting room. I drink tea, listen to music, and strike up a conversation with a woman whose husband is having a triple bypass. Anything to keep my mind occupied. Near the five-hour mark, the Authorized Personnel Only door swings open. Jack stands there in blue scrubs, searching the room.

I hurry over. "Hi, there. How'd surgery go?"

"I got it, Ella. The whole tumor. No surprises. Will did great."

I want to throw my arms around him but not because of the good news. "Can I see him?"

"It's best to wait until tomorrow. He's heavily sedated. I'm transferring him to the ICU shortly."

I breathe in Jack's scent. No aftershave, only soap and perspiration. "What time do you round on patients?"

"Mornings usually, around eight-thirty."

I search for another question to keep him here. "So, you predict a full recovery?"

"The first couple of days will be challenging. I'm optimistic about his long-term prognosis." He squeezes my hand. "I have to go, Ella. I'll keep a close eye on him for you."

Jack disappears behind the secret door where lives are saved and miracles happen. He'll probably change into street clothes and drive home where his wife will greet him with a hug and kiss. The kids will jump into his arms, thrilled to have their dad home. The four of them will sit down for a family dinner and share the highlights of their day.

I, on the other hand, get to return to an overly-scented hotel room for another lonely evening. Or not.

I drive to a nearby park, stick in earbuds, and take off down a trail, breathing in the fresh air. Jack came through for me as I knew he would. He enjoys his career; I can tell by the way his eyes lit up when he talked about the operation. First photography, now medicine. Jack is a man of many talents. Like Leonardo da Vinci.

Oh, my. Talk about purple mountain majesty. The sky transports me to Italy with its pinks, yellows, and oranges. The Rockies are gorgeous. Jack chose a wonderful place to raise his family.

While eating dinner at a Mexican hole-in-the-wall, I check my phone. No messages from the hospital. *Phew!* That means Will is holding his own.

At the hotel I watch the local news then channel surf, searching for a movie. Cable provides hundreds of choices yet nothing appeals to me. Off goes the TV and on comes soothing jazz as I take a long, hot shower.

I climb into bed and turn out the lights. In the darkness, I see Vernazza, the Church of Santa Margherita d'Antiochia, and sapphire eyes penetrating my soul. Why couldn't I have found Jack Thornton first?

FORTY-THREE

A ringing phone wakes me from sleep. "Yes, hello?"
"Hey, girl. Rise and shine. How's the evil one?"

"Tara? What time is it?"

"Six for me; seven for you. How's Will?"

"Sorry I didn't call last night. The surgery went well."

"How long are they keeping him?"

"A week or so."

"And then what?"

It's too early for this. "I'm not sure."

"Be careful, Ella. You're on a slippery slope."

"Well then, I better slide over to the hospital and see what's going on."

"Ha, ha. Very funny. Call me tonight, okay?"

Tara's wake-up call jolts me back to reality. For a heart-stopping moment, I thought the nursing staff was calling about Will. Looks like he made it through the critical first night.

I make tea in the room, then toss it down the drain. The water is filtered through a coffee maker, ruining the taste. I dress, drive to Starbucks, and order an Earl Gray infused with soy. *Mmm,* hot and strong, exactly what I need to face William Walker.

Only the sickest of the sick end up in the ICU and Will is one of them. He's in bed with his eyes closed, bandages spun around his head like a white turban. A dextrose-saline IV replenishes fluids lost during surgery. He's also getting IV antibiotics to stave off infections. A pulse oximeter is clipped to a finger, urine drains into a bag, and wires are taped to his chest and skull. Even though he looks dire, his vital signs are stable.

Someone touches my shoulder. Flutters erupt when Jack smiles, looking clean-shaven and rested. "Morning, Ella. The nurses tell me Will had a good night."

"He's been asleep since I got here. How's the swelling?"

"Let's take a look." Jack washes his hands and pulls on gloves. He shines a penlight in Will's eyes, then uses a small, rubber hammer to test elbow, wrist, knee, and ankle reflexes. Will groans during the exam but doesn't open his eyes.

"Everything looks good. He'll be more alert soon." Jack drops the gloves in the trash. "How was your evening?"

Lonely without you. "Uneventful."

We hold each other's gaze. Jack looks as if he has more to say but holds back. I have questions about Italy yet remain silent. The moment passes.

"Well, I better get to the office." He stops at the nurses' station, types on a computer, and leaves the unit.

I sip my tea, watching Will's heartbeat on a monitor. Six minutes with Jack Thornton stirred more longing than six years with my husband. How will I survive this week?

On the third day, Will is moved to the surgical floor to continue his recovery. His incision shows no sign of infection, and the brain swelling has lessened, both positive signs. He gets irritated easily, especially when he loses a train of thought. He expects me to spend every second with him, forgetting we're in the middle of a divorce.

It's day five, and Jack has arrived for his daily visit. We never talk about anything except Will's progress. I'm having an out-of-body experience watching the two of them interact, or should I say butt heads.

"I thought surgery was supposed to cure these damn headaches," Will grumbles. "I've had one since you operated. Make it stop!"

"Removing the tumor left space that your body must fill," Jack explains for the second time, using slightly different words. "This shift causes discomfort but will end soon. I'll have a nurse bring you pain medication."

"Seriously?" Will folds his arms, looking like a petulant child. "That's the best you got? Choosing between pain or drugs? No wonder there's an opioid crisis."

Jack tosses an empathic look in my direction as he leaves. He'd really feel sorry for me if he knew the whole story.

After an exhausting week, Will and I are flying home. When ten o'clock rolls past, I walk to the nurses' station to find out why Jack hasn't stopped by yet.

"Hi, Becky. When do you expect Doctor Thornton? I have questions about Will's follow-up appointment."

She looks at me with sad, puppy-dog eyes. "He isn't coming in today. Doctor Patel is covering his patients."

My worry antenna shoots up. Jack hasn't missed a single day. "Is he all right?"

Becky zips her lips. "You know HIPAA, Ella."

I spin the bracelet on my wrist, wishing privacy rules didn't apply to me. "I'm wondering if you…"

If what? Ask Jack to stop by so I can steal more minutes with him? Gaze into his eyes one last time? Soak in his scent? No. I must stop pining for what I can never have.

"Will you please thank Doctor Thornton for everything he's done for us?"

I calmly walk to the visitor's bathroom and lock myself in a stall. Not saying goodbye to Jack sends me over the edge. After a cathartic cry, I splash water on my face, press my shoulders back, and return to reality.

Dr. Patel arrives fifteen minutes later, handing me a manila envelope. "Dr. Thornton apologizes for not being here. He made a follow-up appointment for your husband in San Francisco and wanted you to have the medical file."

I bite my tongue so I don't pepper him with questions about Jack's whereabouts.

Dr. Patel examines Will and officially discharges him. Will pitches a fit when an orderly arrives with a wheelchair. "Take that thing away. They operated on my head, not legs."

"Sir, it's our policy to transport patients this way upon leaving the hospital."

"Write new policies."

The orderly looks at me, pleading for help.

Ella to the rescue. "Will, please. We can't go until you sit. It's for your safety."

He tosses the TV remote on the bed and flops down in the chair. "Fine! I'll do anything to get the hell out of here."

I search for Jack in corridors, nursing stations, and patient rooms, vacillating between heartbreak and frustration. He has performed another vanishing act. He knows this is my last day in Colorado. He has my phone number. How much effort does it take to call or text? Then again, disappearing is his modus operandi. *Goodbye, Dr. Thornton. Have a good life.*

FORTY-FOUR

Traveling with Will is like caring for abandoned puppies—except the puppies behave better. He requires constant attention and does nothing to help himself. He complains about the bus ride from the rental car building to the airport (too hot, bad driver), the security line (too long, he had to remove his shoes), and the connector train ride to Terminal C (too bumpy and crowded).

"Why can't the idiots who run this place buy comfortable chairs?" Will stretches out across four seats. "Get me a beer to numb the pain."

Sitting next to him on a packed plane tests my resolve. I let the flight attendants deal with him. Even though Will is exhausted after landing in California, he refuses to ride in a wheelchair or take one of those zippy golf carts. Instead, we walk to the long-term parking lot, which tires him even more.

He slides into the passenger seat. "This car sucks. When are you getting a new one?"

"Please buckle your seatbelt."

"You sound like those glorified waitresses up in the sky. Buckle up, stay seated, turn off your phone, don't—"

"I get it, Will." I glance at his bandage, reminding me not to snap. This has been a grueling day for him. Once we're on the freeway, I brace myself for the next battle.

"You living alone right now is a bad idea. Can your mom or brother help out?"

"Drop it, Ella."

"What about Jenna? You two seem to get along. Maybe she'll stay with you."

"Quit orchestrating my goddamn life! Take me home and fuck off!"

Baiting him with Jenna was a lousy idea. "You need help, Will. Food, cleaning, shopping, driving."

"You stay if you're so worried."

I knew this would happen. "Fine, but only until your neuro appointment. After that, you're on your own."

"Whatever makes you happy, Saint Ella." He lays back and closes his eyes.

It's not you!

I take a deep breath to calm myself. We've come this far. I might as well see him cross the finish line. It's only two weeks. Once he gets a clean bill of health, I'm washing my hands of William Walker for good.

No matter what happens.

Forever and ever.

Yeah, right.

The Mill Valley house officially belongs to Will, and as I look back, it always has. He pressured me to buy it; I wanted a smaller, less expensive home. The flat-screen TV and Bose soundbar overpowers the living room. Even the brown-hued master bedroom suits a man more than a woman.

Will goes straight to the fridge, opens a beer, and sits in front of the television with his remote. The place is a disaster. Dust, beer bottles, and coffee mugs are scattered throughout the house. Dishes clutter the sink; the hamper is overflowing.

During the next week, I cook, clean, and work in the garden while Will heals from surgery. I lock the guest room door at night to ensure my safety. He's getting stronger—and more belligerent—each passing day. He brings up me lying about the birthday party, escaping to Italy—all the old arguments.

After a brutal week, it's time for a break. I drive to Piedmont to check on my home, then meet Tara for lunch. The afternoon passes quickly, and soon I'm returning to Mill Valley with three grocery bags. I hope Will didn't drink booze while I was gone. I don't want him tripping and injuring himself. He's tired of me hovering, and I'm ready to go home. His appointment can't come soon enough for either of us.

I'm surprised to see a second BMW parked in the driveway. Will didn't say anything about visitors. Luckily, there's street parking close by. I set the groceries on the kitchen table and go exploring. No one is in the living room. Nothing happening in the guest bathroom or home office. The television is blaring in the master bedroom. I walk in and freeze. Will and Jenna are fooling around in bed.

Jenna pulls up a sheet as if covering herself makes a difference.

"Uh, sorry," Will says, not looking sorry at all. "Thought your gab session with the obnoxious one would last longer."

He's not worthy of a response. I turn off the TV. "Nice to see you again, Jenna. Guess he's all yours now."

She turns away, unable to hold eye contact. I'm surprised she hasn't minded me staying here, given their relationship. Will links his hands behind his neck, grinning. He's enjoying the drama, manipulating her as much as me. What little compassion I had for him ends now. He has me cooking and cleaning, and her making booty calls.

I focus on Jenna. "There's food in the kitchen for dinner. Make sure Will takes his meds. His neuro appointment is on Thursday. Don't miss it. The rest is up to you." I do an about-face and walk away; my doormat days are over.

"Come on, Ella, don't be pissed." Will scrambles into his pants and follows me down the hallway. "You're the one who filed for divorce!"

I throw my things in a suitcase. "What you do with Jenna or anyone else is not my concern. Your house, your life. Live as you wish. I'm going home."

"But... I need help! Your words, not mine. Jenna works long hours. She doesn't have time for this. All you do is sit on your ass."

What? Did he really say that after what I've sacrificed for him? I swing open the door and go outside before I punch him in the nose.

He grabs my arm. "You owe me, Ella."

I yank free. "I owe you nothing! Don't ever touch or call me again. It's over."

"You bet it's over." He sneers. "Who wants a barren slut hanging around anyway? Jenna's pregnant. You caught us celebrating. At least she's woman enough to carry my kid."

Tears spring to my eyes. Just when I think he can't get any meaner, he hurls those hurtful words, knowing how much children mean to me. He's standing there gloating, proud of himself for knocking me down once again.

Then, the most surprising thing happens, a watershed moment. I notice he's not wearing a shirt, his jeans are barely zipped, and he's shoeless. Loverboy is barefoot and pregnant! The cliché cracks me up. My cackles turn into a belly laugh. I double over, releasing one snort after another as I visualize him with a swollen stomach about to give birth.

"Get off *my* property, you crazy bitch!" He hurls more profanity but his hate-filled words blow past like feathers in the wind. I drive away without any guilt or obligation, my penance complete. Jenna McQuinn is the best thing that has ever happened to me. I'm free!

FORTY-FIVE

Taking care of Will has drained me. I sleep nine, ten hours a night, plus naps. Every day, I power walk in my neighborhood to restore my energy.

Susan and Ollie are glad I'm home. She invited me to play bunco but I'm not ready to take Mom's place at the table. It's nice having a neighbor who cares about me, though.

Will's neuro appointment was yesterday. I'm tempted to call and learn how he's doing but don't. I'm sure he's fine. Otherwise, he or Jenna would've called. I'm fixing lunch when my phone rings. *Ugh.* Area code 720. The accounting office in Boulder better not be calling again about Will's hospital bill.

"Hello?"

"Hello, back. It's Jack Thornton. Did I catch you at a good time?"

I almost drop the phone.

"Ella? Are you there?"

"Yes. Just surprised to hear from you."

"Yesterday was Will's appointment. How's he doing?"

I can't believe he tracked the date. "I don't know, Jack. I wasn't there. You'll have to call him."

"It sounds as if you're not living together."

"We've been separated since I returned from Italy. I was helping him get through surgery but things got complicated."

"How so?"

"Nothing about his health, just personal stuff." *Time to redirect.* "How's work? Are the wife and kids keeping you busy?"

"Ella? He lowers his voice. "Why would you mention my wife?"

"Come on, Jack. I saw her picture on your desk. At least I know why you ditched me in Italy."

"What are you talking about?"

"Breakfast in Vernazza? You were a no-show?"

Silence.

"Jack?"

"I think I solved the mystery. You never got my letter, did you?"

"What are you talking about?"

"I wrote a letter explaining why I left the Cinque Terre so abruptly."

"No, Jack. I never got it. I looked everywhere for you. I went to your village and knocked on so many doors. You simply vanished."

"I didn't vanish, Ella. The reason I left is part of a longer story. Would you like to hear it?"

I sit on the sofa, my nerve endings on edge. "Very much so."

FORTY-SIX

"My wife died in childbirth, Ella." She developed severe pre-eclampsia at twenty-nine weeks. I won't go into details but Charlotte passed away during an emergency cesarean. That photo on my desk is the last one I have of her."

His voice is filled with gut-wrenching emotion.

"My daughter almost didn't make it. She spent months in the NICU before coming home. I noticed delays in reaching milestones such as rolling over, sitting, crawling. Her pediatrician diagnosed cerebral palsy."

"Rose had a grand mal seizure and was hospitalized when I was in Italy. My dad called in the middle of the night to tell me. I had to get to her, Ella. If I didn't take the early-morning train to Florence, I would've missed the only flight home. I wrote a letter explaining this to you. I described where you were staying as best I could. The hotel owner promised to deliver it."

My heart aches for his unimaginable pain. "How's Rose now?"

"Not good. She had another seizure the morning you and Will left Colorado. We're trying different meds to stabilize her."

Jack's life is nothing as I imagined. The pressure on him boggles my mind. "How were you able to get away to Italy with so much going on?"

No response, only a tired sigh.

"I apologize, Jack. That's none of my business."

"It's a fair question. Rose turned three on June twenty-six. Celebrating her birthday also means mourning my wife's death. Those gray clouds were hard to shake this year, especially with Charlotte's parents staying with us. My sister signed me up for a medical conference in Florence. I wasn't allowed to come home without photos from there and the Cinque Terre."

The sadness in his voice breaks my heart. Jack is such a strong, capable man. His depression must have been severe for his family to intervene.

"Leaving the kids was difficult but Julia was right. I wasn't functioning very well. Anyway, I'm better now." He clears his throat. "Before hanging up there's something I want to say. Not about Charlotte or the kids. About us. If it makes you uncomfortable, I'll stop. It's been a while since—"

"Jack! Just say it."

"I'm drawn to you, Ella. A visceral pull that keeps me awake at night. I felt it in Italy. I felt it in Colorado. I feel it now. Do you"—he catches his breath—"feel the same way about me?"

Shockwaves ripple through my body. "Oh, Jack, you have no idea. I feel our connection even when we're *not* together."

"You mean that?"

"Every word."

"Well then, let's do something about it. I owe you breakfast."

I'm weeping with joy, wanting to kick myself for not discussing what happened in Italy when we had the chance. "What'd you have in mind?"

"We'll have to get creative given our living situations. Let's toss out ideas and see what sticks."

Jack doesn't want to involve the kids, and I want to protect my privacy. We decide to meet on neutral ground: Sedona, Arizona, a place on both of our bucket lists. Once he's confident Rose's new meds are working, we'll slip away for a long weekend. Meanwhile, we agree to text every day and share one fact about ourselves as a way to stay connected.

"Well, duty calls," Jack says. "I'm sorry about Italy, Ella. I promise to make amends."

"Your touch, your voice, your eyes. If you knew how you affected me, you'd think I was a love-struck girl instead of a thirty-year-old woman."

He chuckles. "You sure know how to brighten a guy's day. Oh, and by the way, Will is doing fine in case you're wondering. His San Francisco doctor called yesterday with an update. *Arrivederci, bella signorina.*"

FORTY-SEVEN

I knew it! Jack and I are soulmates. His ability to speak from the heart and his devotion to family touch a place deep inside me. And I love his playfulness. He isn't arrogant. That man is feisty!

Such random events have led me to him. Where would I be had I not stayed in Vernazza? What if I hadn't helped that kid on the trail or ventured out to Manarola for dinner? What if I'd refused to help Will?

I think about the grotto in Italy where I had a spiritual experience, sensing a High Power guiding my life. It's happening again. How else do you explain what just unfolded?

I step over to a window. "Hello, up there. You've made me a happy woman today. While I don't understand Your ways, why You led Jack and me on such a twisty path, it's not important. What matters is where we ended up. If it's okay with You, I'll take the reins from here. No more surprises."

An otherworldly sensation prickles my skin followed by a gust of warmth. A Higher Power's approval? My blissful state? Does it matter? I'm going to Sedona with my soulmate!

Our daily texting game reveals a lot about Jack's values, personality, and quirks. He neither shares much information nor struggles with ambiguity. He views life in well-defined terms, much like Tara. He's serious most of the time, sliding in humor when I least expect it. I can't wait to see how he tops his ninth response on this list.

Ella

1. I've been a NICU nurse for five years. I'm currently unemployed (My choice; I didn't get fired). I'm pondering two job options.
2. I'm an only child. My dad passed away just after I turned twelve. Mom recently died of pancreatic cancer. I miss them so much.
3. I live in my childhood home. The town (Piedmont) is named after a region in Italy. Fun fact, right?
4. Mexican is my favorite food (FYI: Margaritas are considered essential food).
5. My best friend is Tara Collins. I love her more than life itself. Don't <u>ever</u> make me choose between you and her (that's a joke but please don't make me choose).
6. If everyone soaked in lavender baths by candlelight, we'd have world peace. (BTW, I liked the lavender scent on your skin in Italy. I'm blushing. Are you?).
7. I enjoy listening to music more than watching TV. I have different playlists on my phone, depending on my mood. (But I'm NOT a moody person!).
8. Christmas is my favorite holiday. The whole season is magical. I hope you decorate your house (and the tree MUST be real, never fake!).
9. I fixed a leaky faucet, put shelves on a wall, and painted my bedroom. I've never done maintenance work so it's a big deal. I'm turning into a handywoman. Did my spin on words make you smile?

10. I'll hike anywhere, anytime. Nature centers me. Did you know Sedona has fantastic trails?

<u>Jack</u>
1. I enjoy living in my cabin with the kids.
2. Lucas and Rose are priorities.
3. I don't cook but I like to barbecue.
4. Fly-fishing and photography are two hobbies.
5. I like evenings at home rather than going out.
6. I prefer casual clothes over suits.
7. My dad is a retired cardiologist, my role model.
8. My sister Julia is my best friend.
9. I'm crushing on a girl from California.

Chime. A text from Jack!
   #10 *Ready to pack your bags?*
I call him immediately. "Does this mean Rose is better?"
"I'm pleased to report the new meds are working."
"No more seizures?"
"Nope. It's time to focus on us."
"When can you get away?"
"How about this Friday, October seventh? For three nights?"
His words ignite sparks. "My calendar is wide open."
"Ella, about our sleeping arrangements. Do you have a preference? I know what I want."
An involuntary moan escapes. "It doesn't matter where we stay as long as we're together."
"Okay, then. I'll make a reservation."
My heart is skipping all over the place. "What time are you arriving?"

"Southwest Airlines has many flights into Phoenix. I found one from Denver that lands at eleven-thirty and one from Oakland at eleven-forty. Both have return flights close to four."

"It's perfect. Let's book our own flight, you find the room, and I'll reserve a rental car."

"Good plan. And, Ella? I'm looking forward to our time together. I'll see you in Phoenix."

I'm breathless after our call ends. Never in my wildest dreams did I imagine someone like Jack Thornton—and everything that comes with him—would fill the longing in my heart.

It's time to tell Tara about Jack. Over dinner at my house, she learns my secret. I didn't get the reaction I expected.

"From where I sit, this trip feels rushed," she says. "You barely know the guy. What's the hurry?"

"He and I share something special. Please trust me, okay?"

"Trust has nothing to do with it, Ella. You just ended things with Will. Take a minute to catch your breath before launching into another relationship."

"After meeting Jack, you'll know why I'm going to Sedona. He's the one, Tara. He's my person."

She rolls her eyes. "If I had a buck for every client who regretted saying that, I'd own a Nob Hill mansion."

I'm unsure how to respond. After all, my marriage proves her point. But I'm not giving up on love. Finding that special someone is like traveling to Vernazza from California. It's an arduous journey but worth the sacrifice once you arrive.

After Tara goes home, I mosey to my bedroom. What should I wear in Sedona? I'm tempted to run out and buy new clothes. I end up packing items from my closet. This weekend isn't about outward appearances.

I wonder about a small gift for Jack. Maybe lavender soap? My face warms as I imagine giving it to him.

FORTY-EIGHT

I arrive at the Oakland airport wearing jeans, hiking boots, and a cream-colored sweater/hat combo. Sitting is impossible; I'm too wound up about seeing Jack. I walk around the terminal to release energy.

Other than the jet taking off six minutes late, it's an uneventful flight. We're descending into Phoenix, my leg bouncing like a pogo stick. It's interesting how random thoughts worm their way inside one's mind. Right now, the Italian massage is entertaining me. I remember how my body responded to the masseuse's touch. Will Jack affect me the same way?

The plane lurches to a halt and rolls to a gate. People spill into the middle aisle, gathering their items from overhead bins. *Come on, come one, come on.* I hurry down the jetway, feeling like a kid waking up on Christmas morning.

My gift from Santa is standing off to the left, smiling. Those sapphire eyes probe as I get close. "Good flight?" His lips brush mine, sending goosebumps down my spine.

"Yes, thanks." I squeeze his hand, making sure he's real. I can't believe we're here as a couple.

We retrieve our luggage and board a van that shuttles us to a rental car lot where a Subaru Forester is waiting. As we begin the two-hour drive to Sedona, there's a distance—an awkwardness—between us. We're talking but it's stilted.

"Pull over, please."

"What?"

"Pull over and stop the car."

He eases to the side of the road, his brow wrinkled. "What's going on, Ella?"

I hold his face, using my thumbs to massage his cheeks. "Being together—anticipating this weekend—is nerve-racking for me. I imagine it's that way for you, too. I want nothing to come between us. Let's savor each moment, beginning now." I kiss those soft lips.

"I feel better. How about you?"

A slow smile builds as he continues driving, the invisible barrier gone. He talks about Lucas and Rose and his life in Colorado. I describe growing up in the Bay Area and tell him about Tara, Mom, and anything else that comes to mind.

As we approach Sedona, Jack points at the red mountains. "The sun is supposed to change their color throughout the day. I'm looking forward to capturing it on camera." He glances at me. "What's on your list?"

"The obvious activity is hiking. Trails are everywhere. Boynton Canyon and Bell Mountain have an energy field called a vortex I want to experience. Also, I found a church I think you'll like."

"Sounds good." He clasps my hand. "You'll like where we're staying." His expression hints at a few surprises.

FORTY-NINE

Excitement builds as we leave the highway and weave several miles through the backroads toward our hotel. If it wasn't for signage, I'd swear the GPS was taking us in the wrong direction.

The Enchantment Resort is painted red like the rocks, making it an extension of Boynton Canyon. The remote location offers seclusion from the rest of the world, a perfect romantic getaway.

A man in a guard shack welcomes us and provides directions to the check-in office. An attentive bellhop escorts us to our room, or should I say suite. The living room has a wood-beam ceiling, a gas fireplace, a sofa, and a dining table next to a kitchenette. Our bathroom has a free-standing tub, a walk-in shower, and double vanity. There's a separate bedroom with a sliding glass door that opens onto a private deck.

"Thanks for finding such a special place for us, Jack."

He folds me in his arms. "You're welcome. I'm ordering refreshments. What would you like?"

"Pinot Grigio is my favorite wine."

Drinks, cheese, crackers, and fruit are delivered by the time we freshen up and unpack our suitcases. Jack carries the wine bottle and two glasses to the deck; I follow with the food platter.

We nestle together on a cushioned sofa, soaking in the landscape. Jack breaks the comfortable silence. "I'm glad you had me stop the car on the way here."

"What makes you say that?"

"I am anxious about this weekend." He massages my hand with his thumb. "I haven't been with anyone since Charlotte."

I sit up, wondering if I heard correctly. "So, coming here with me is a big deal."

He nods, swishing wine in his glass. "I'm curious. What are your plans now that Will is out of the picture?"

I gaze at him, batting my eyelashes. "Spending quality time with you."

He delivers a half-smile and waits for more. My travel buddy isn't letting me off the hook. I drain my wine glass for liquid courage. It's time for full disclosure.

"Before talking about the future, I want to share two things from the past. In my early twenties, I was diagnosed with ovarian cancer and had a hysterectomy. If you want more children, I'm willing to adopt but can't give you a child."

I take an extra breath. "I also want you to know that Will abused me. Emotionally and physically. Tara took me to Italy after a particularly bad incident. It's why I stayed two extra weeks in Vernazza. It's also why I clammed up that night in the church. The abuse was too raw to discuss back then."

Jack shakes his head. "I'm sorry he hurt you, Ella."

"I'm sorry I let him." I pop berries in my mouth. "Looking forward, I'm really just trying to find my footing. My divorce will be final next March. I'm exploring job opportunities that push me out of my comfort zone. And I'm not sure about living long term in Mom's house; it's a lot to manage. Other than wanting to travel more, that's what's on my mind. I probably sound vague, but this is where I am."

"You don't sound vague at all. You're starting over, figuring out what's right for you."

"That I am." I feed him a berry. "May I put you on the hot seat?"

He smiles. "Ask away."

"You mentioned being anxious about this weekend. Is it only because of your celibacy? Or is there more?"

Jack eats cheese and a cracker. "It's more." He gazes into the distance. "A lot of anxiety comes from the fact I'm a package deal. Anyone I bring into my life also enters my children's."

He shifts his stare at me. "I must be careful."

Those piercing eyes make me squirm. Is he worried about my past? Does he think I'll be a bad influence on his kids?

He raises my chin until we're at eye level. "Ella, you are the first woman since Charlotte who gives me hope that all three of us can fall in love again."

What? Did he really just say that? I choke back tears. "Oh, Jack. That's the nicest thing anyone has ever said to me."

He traces my lips with his thumb. "Back in Portofino. When you put two spoons in one cup. That's when I knew."

"Knew what?"

"That I wanted you."

I lean into his touch. "I'm yours, Jack. All of me."

He sets his wine glass down, stands, and pulls me in his arms, kissing me with an urgency that matches my own. We stumble into the bedroom, caressing each other. He slides my sweater over my head, stroking my skin and freeing my bra. Our breathing quickens when his lips find my breasts. His touch is exquisite.

I peel off his sweater and T-shirt, stroking his chest. The desire in his eyes—and elsewhere—grows. He moves us to the bed. I wiggle out of my jeans and panties, kicking them to the floor. He finishes undressing and slides in beside me. We're ready to explode, yet he takes his time, kissing my eyes, cheeks, nose, and mouth. "You're a beautiful woman, Ella, inside and out. I'm so glad I found you."

His words send me over the edge. Our desire turns into fiery passion as we become one. Nothing matters except him and this moment. My body shatters into an intense orgasm, wave after wave of indescribable pleasure. He follows with a powerful release, our chests rising and falling in tandem. We lie face to face, waiting for our breathing to return to normal.

"I knew it'd be like this," Jack murmurs. "I knew making love with you would be the most natural thing in the world." We kiss, whispering tender words. "Let's spoon. There's something I want you to see."

"Spoon?"

"Close your eyes." He gently turns me away from him, then pulls my body into his, molding us together like spoons in a drawer. "Open them."

I peer through the glass door, gasping at the beauty. "It's a living fresco, Jack." I relax in his embrace, watching the sunset paint the canyon dazzling colors. Never in my life have I felt such contentment.

"Want to get ready for dinner?" He kisses my shoulder as the sun fades.

"Do you mind if we order room service? I don't want to leave this bed for the rest of the night."

FIFTY

I wake with the sunrise, feeling tired, cherished, and happier than I have ever been in my life. Jack rolls up on his elbow and tickles my nose with my hair. "Pretty amazing first night, I'd say. Shall we get up and see what Sedona's like outside our room?"

"I'm content to stay in this bed all three days." I trace his lips with my finger, my heart bursting with love.

"We'll return soon enough." He raises his chin toward the window. "Light's good for photography. Let's get cleaned up and hike the canyon, take pictures. Afterward, we'll drive to town for breakfast."

"That chapel isn't too far from downtown."

"Looks like we have a plan."

My travel book says Sedona is a sacred place, a cathedral without walls. A mysterious cosmic force is said to emanate from its red rocks, creating swirling energy known as a vortex. There are four sites where the energy is supposed to crackle more intensely; Boynton Canyon is one. I'm about to find out if it's true.

We walk a short distance from the hotel to the Boynton Canyon Trail where astonishing views are everywhere. Five hot air balloons float silently across the valley, playing tag with one another. We hike in and out of shadows, tiny lizards rustling in the brush, songbirds answering one another's call. We follow signs to the vista, saving the longer route for later.

We arrive at the end of a box canyon and climb a massive sandstone rock. It's a challenging ascent, not for the faint of heart. Jack adjusts his camera's settings as I make my way to the Kachina Woman, a tall, rounded spire with a sphinx-like head. I find a comfortable place to sit at her base and close my eyes, taking deep breaths to clear my mind. The sun warms my face. A plane hums in the distance. Birds chirp all around me. Other hikers walk by, whispering. Wind whistles through trees. Breathe in, out, in, out. Let all thoughts go.

A vibration emanates from inside my body—or maybe it's from the ground, I'm not sure. The sensation is subtle, powerful, otherworldly. I'm one with the mountains, cactus, trees, and birds. No more, no less as we coexist on the planet. Time passes.

I feel a presence and open my eyes. Jack is standing several yards away, watching me. When I return his smile, he walks over, holding out a hand to help me up. "Well? Did you feel the vortex?"

His touch ignites a heightened sense of belonging, more meaningful than a brief dance with Mother Earth. "Yes, and he's fantastic."

We retrace our steps to the resort and drive to town for breakfast. Afterward, we stroll along the main street, passing souvenir, crystal, and fudge shops. Clothing boutiques. Arts and crafts and jewelry stores. Jack squeezes my hand after seven or eight minutes. "Ready to find the chapel?"

I don't think my love is much of a window-shopper.

Eleven minutes out of town, we spot a ninety-foot cross chiseled between towering peaks two hundred feet above the ground. Jack's camera is clicking as we hike up a steep road from a parking lot.

The Chapel of the Holy Cross is a tiny hilltop church with only seven pews on each side. It's a perfect balance of religious simplicity and nature. I light a candle in my mother's memory, wishing she had met Jack. She would have loved him as much as me.

"Ella? Come see this view."

I slide my arm around his waist as we stand in front of a floor-to-ceiling window overlooking the Sedona Valley. Soaring red monoliths dot the terraced landscape as far as the eye can see. I gesture across the terrain. "That looks like Bell Mountain. Want to check it out since we're so close?"

He murmurs in my ear, "I'd rather return to our room."

Oh, my. Who needs another vortex when you have Jack Thornton?"

FIFTY-ONE

B ack in our suite, Jack wraps his arms around me. "Would you like to soak in the tub?"

I nod eagerly. This man is full of surprises. He's not too affectionate in public, yet once we're alone that changes. Life with Will was the opposite. Outward appearances—what others saw—mattered the most.

"Give me a minute." Jack disappears into the bathroom.

I remove my hiking boots and set out the lavender soap, hoping to weave some fun into his plan.

He returns with a sensual smile. A moan slips from my throat as he peels away my clothing, touching me wherever he wants. My breathing quickens after undressing him, running my fingers through his coarse chest hair. His body is a new trail and I'm an eager explorer.

He leads me to the tub where flickering candles cast a romantic aura on the walls, a fantasy plucked straight from my mind. He steps through the scented foam, bringing me with him. I lie against his chest, closing my eyes. His fingers trace my inner thighs, move to my stomach, and settle on my breasts. He makes me feel desired, uninhibited, safe.

I lift the lavender soap. "May I wash you?"

"Be my guest." I maneuver around in the tub, massaging his neck, shoulders, chest, and arms. I take my time, wanting him to feel as cherished as he makes me feel.

He opens his eyes halfway. "Are you always this way? So easy to be with?"

Every moment with him is a journey, discovering depths I never knew existed. "I could ask you the same question."

We dry off, fall into bed, and make unhurried love.

Later, we dress in robes and sit on the sofa, chatting about mundane things, although nothing about Jack is ordinary. In the late afternoon, he glances at a clock. "Please excuse me."

"Calling home?"

He nods. "I want to check on the kids."

"You don't have to leave for that." I pat the space beside me, hoping he returns to the couch. I want him to feel comfortable taking care of responsibilities when we're together.

"See how easy you make things?" He dials Julia's number and begins speaking in a relaxed tone. As the kids come on the line, he holds the phone between us, letting me hear the conversation.

"Well?" he says after ending the call. "How was your intro to my kiddos?"

I'm amazed by how lovingly he speaks with his family. I press my hand over his heart. "Those sweet kids hit the dad lottery."

My heart warms knowing I'm becoming part of his world.

FIFTY-TWO

Jack and I hike, photograph the mountains, eat southwestern food, and find new ways to make love. We create our own Sedona cocoon.

We splurge for dinner at a trendy restaurant called Elote on our last evening. We begin with an appetizer of roasted corn with spicy mayo, lime, and cheese served with homemade tortilla chips, and end with slow-cooked carnitas for me and salmon mole for Jack.

When we return to the resort, our bed has been turned down, romantic music is playing, and flames are flickering in the gas fireplace. Chilled champagne and chocolate-covered strawberries are on the table.

Tears spring to my eyes. "When did you have time to arrange this?"

"It's part of the honeymoon package." He pours two glasses of champagne, handing one to me. "To us. To our beginning."

We lounge in robes on the outside deck in the morning, sipping hot beverages and listening to a far-off flute sound. Native Americans play music every sunrise, sending love and peace into the world.

I wiggle Jack's pinky. "I officially forgive you for ditching me in Italy."

"Well, I don't forgive the woman who ran the hotel where I stayed. I gave her fifty euros to find you."

We have a good laugh, stretching out the time before packing up and driving to Phoenix to catch our flights.

"You're quiet," Jack says after entering city limits. He pulls my hand on his lap. "Everything okay?"

"I can't imagine waking up without you."

He caresses my hand with his thumb. "Same for me."

"What's our next step, Jack? Where do we go from here?"

"I've been thinking about that. Thanksgiving week is coming up; the kids are out of school. How'd you like to meet them? Stay with us?"

I squeeze his hand. "There's nothing I'd rather do."

Jack parks in the rental car lot. As we shuttle to the terminal, I struggle not to cry. He and I have been through so much. I'm afraid if he leaves, I'll never see him again.

After navigating through security, Jack studies the electronic board. "My flight's leaving first; you have time to walk me to the gate."

Passengers are already lining up to board his jet. Jack hustles me to a corner. I pucker up, preparing for a goodbye kiss. Instead, he bypasses my lips and whispers in my ear, "You have been a *fantastic* photo assistant. I can't wait to work with you again if you catch my drift."

A strange laugh/cry escapes from my throat. No mushy stuff from this guy. I throw my arms around his neck. "I'll miss you, Jack Thornton. I'll never have enough days with you."

He uses his thumbs to wipe away my tears. "We'll video chat and text. Thanksgiving will be here before you know it."

The gate agent calls for final boarding. One last hug and Jack disappears in the jetway, ending our fantasy weekend. When I'm in his arms, anything seems possible. Watching his jet pull away from the terminal returns me to reality. He's entrenched in Colorado whereas I'm a native Californian. Is there a way to merge our lives? Or are we destined to live separately, held together by romantic getaways and holiday visits? How is this long-distance relationship suppose to work?

FIFTY-THREE

I return home from Sedona and settle into a routine with one major difference: life is rainy-day gray instead of double rainbows without Jack. I think about him constantly until I realize what I'm doing.

I'm on this journey with a man I love, waiting for a Cinderella ending. I lost my identity once by following in Will's shadow; I don't want that to happen with Jack. I remove my head from the clouds and get busy.

The first item on my list is to respond to a letter I received from Doctors Without Borders. Apparently, they liked my resume. During a phone interview, I learn the organization sends healthcare professionals around the world to deliver medical care to vulnerable people. My NICU background is of high interest to them. The director asks me to come in for a panel interview but I decline. Why waste their time? I want a life with Jack.

But how do I make that transition?

I might as well accept the fact that I'm relocating, not him. Even though we've fast-tracked our relationship by going to Sedona, we're still getting to know each other. I think travel nursing is the best fit for me. That way, I can work around Jack's schedule, allowing us to spend chunks of time together. After the holidays, I'll call the agency and sign a contract. With luck, my first assignment will be in Boulder.

Meanwhile, I want to keep busy. Mom served at the local food pantry; I might as well keep the goodness going. I meet with the director who welcomes me aboard. I devote four hours every Monday and Thursday to packing and distributing food. I'm surprised by the number of working poor who stop by. One woman juggles two jobs to support her family and still struggles to put enough food on the table. I've shied away from politics, but someone has to engage with elected officials about the minimum wage crisis.

Lunching with my former colleagues is a treat. When I lived with Will, he guilted me every time I went out with friends, saying I stole hours from him. Over time, I stopped seeing everyone except Tara. I'm glad those days are behind me. I haven't heard a peep from him since the blow-up at his house. I dread the day he learns about Jack and me. Explaining our relationship will be tricky.

Handling home business has consumed considerable time. I'm embarrassed to admit I have never paid household bills, having gone from living at home (where Mom took care of everything) to marriage (where I gave my paycheck to Will). I'm becoming comfortable with e-banking and have set up autopay. I've also linked expenses like insurance and cable to my credit card. Managing my finances is not only empowering but it's easier than Will led me to believe.

Tara's law practice keeps growing, forcing her to work longer hours. We managed to fit in a couple of meals where I told her about Sedona. Of course, she had already Googled Jack's name and knew about his education, career, etcetera. She even knew about Charlotte, thanks to an online obituary. I almost wish I hadn't read it.

Jack's wife grew up in upstate New York, the daughter of a judge (mom) and an architect (dad). She was a music prodigy, graduating from Juilliard. She and Jack met when her quartet played at a fundraiser for his medical school. Charlotte left the quartet to join the

Boulder Symphony while Jack finished his fellowship at Cornell. They were building a life together when Charlotte unexpectedly died, leaving him with two kids and a broken heart.

For couples who divorce like Will and me, moving on is easy. Searching for a better future propels us forward. Losing someone in the middle of a love story binds the survivor to memories and what-might-have-been dreams. How do I compete with that?

Tara tells me not to compare myself with Charlotte, to focus on building my relationship with Jack. Her advice keeps me grounded. We'll see how my efforts play out when I fly to Colorado tomorrow. It's been six long weeks since Sedona. I'm more than ready to see Jack in person.

I want to bring gifts for Lucas and Rose, something meaningful. Inspiration hits when I find two beloved books on a shelf: *The Growing Tree* by Shel Silverstein and *The Very Hungry Caterpillar* by Eric Carle. I will share a part of me with the kids by giving them these childhood treasures.

Jack's present is a photograph of us on a Sedona trail. I hope the brushed-nickel frame matches his home decor.

With gifts wrapped and clothes packed, I'm ready to visit my love on his turf. Texting and video chats have only deepened our relationship. I haven't had any contact with the kids, however. Jack called them a package deal. Will I bond with his little ones? Do I have what it takes to be a mother?

I'm about to find out.

FIFTY-FOUR

Jack asked me to text him for a curbside pick-up. I'm surprised when he pulls up in a silver Jeep with a Golden Retriever instead of two kids.

He hops out, smiling. "Hi, there."

I wrap my arms around his neck. "I've missed you!"

A whimper comes from the rear seat. "Who's your friend?"

"Meet Ruby. She snuck in when I wasn't looking."

Jack loads my suitcase in the Jeep. He's wearing jeans, a denim shirt, and brown western boots. A Stetson covers a child's booster chair in the back seat. I've met the hiker/photographer, the neurosurgeon, and now the rancher/father. His latest role makes me love him most of all.

"You're sexy in those boots, cowboy."

He shakes his head. "Let's get you home."

He hands me a thermos. "We're at fifty-four hundred feet. You might have shortness of breath, dry skin, or disruptive sleep the first night or two. It's good to hydrate."

I sip cold water, watching him from the corner of my eye. "Do you take care of everyone this well?"

"I do my best."

The highway brings us close to the foothills. The outside temperature is a cool forty-three degrees; the day is crisp and clear. Clouds hover in the unreal blue sky.

"Tell me more about the ranch."

"Well, my family has lived in a rural part of Boulder County for over a century. We're ten miles north of Boulder and twenty-three miles east of Rocky Mountain National Park. The ranch is closest to the town of Lyons."

"Must be nice having such deep roots. Does Julia live there, also?"

"No. She and her husband have a place in Denver. Dave's an accountant; Jules teaches fourth grade. My folks live in my grandparents' house." He taps the steering wheel with his thumb. "Charlotte and I built the cabin after we married. I've thought about moving because of the memories but the kids love living there." He gazes out his side window.

Whenever Jack mentions his wife, he gets so sad. I might as well address the elephant in the car. "Is it hard for you to bring another woman to the cabin?"

He taps the steering wheel again.

"It's okay to talk about her, Jack. Charlotte will always be part of your life because of Lucas and Rose. And I'm grateful you found room for me."

"You have an uncanny ability to read my mind." He pulls my hand in his lap and kisses it. "I better be careful."

He turns off I-36 onto a paved road. Trees with orange, yellow, and red leaves line a creek, its water flowing around rocks and fallen branches. Jack raises his chin at a two-story house across a field. "My folks live over there."

The property has a barn and several outbuildings. Black and white cows are grazing in a fenced area. We pass a herd of black cattle spread out on the open range. Ruby stands and whimpers after we turn on a gravel road.

"This is my place."

The house's exterior resembles a log cabin but that's where the similarity ends. His home is a modern, two-story with a dark green roof, three chimneys, a wrap-around porch, and a three-car garage. There's a massive wooden play structure with swings, a slide, a rock-climbing wall, and a fort in the side yard. A netted trampoline is nearby. Horses are nibbling hay outside a barn; chickens are scratching in a coop.

"Some cabin," I say, trying to contain the flutters in my stomach.

He parks in the garage and opens Ruby's door. She runs into the yard as Jack leads me into his life.

FIFTY-FIVE

"Ready for a quick tour?" Jack brings my suitcase inside. "The main floor has a kitchen, living room, dining room, library, and half-bath." He gestures to an area behind us. "A laundry room and pantry are over there."

The home has quality touches everywhere. High ceilings give it an open, airy feel. Tubular skylights brighten the kitchen's granite island and farmhouse sink. Copper-bottomed pots and pans dangle above a six-burner stove. A stylish breakfast nook with bench seating is tucked next to a bow window.

The formal dining room seats eight, the furniture blending seamlessly with the log-cabin design. A fireplace between the dining and living rooms heats both ways.

What catches my eye is an enormous picture window that showcases a backyard meadow and the Rockies. I step closer to admire the view. "You did a great job bringing the outside into the house."

He wraps his arms around me from behind, laying his chin on my shoulder. "Glad you like it." Soon, he's kissing my neck.

I turn around. "Lucas and Rose. Are they here?"

"No, they're with my folks." His eyes twinkle with mischief. "I wanted time alone with you."

I slip my finger through his belt loop and tug him closer. "And why is that?"

"Too many windows down here to show you." He scoops up my hand and leads me up a wide staircase.

We enter a family room built around a wood-burning fireplace. It has a kid-sized table and chairs, a painting/chalkboard easel, a piano keyboard, a recliner, and an L-shaped sofa. Built-in shelving is jammed with books, photographs, and board games. There's a bay window with cushioned seating next to a roll-top desk.

Lucas's bedroom is painted light blue with an astronomy motif. "He sees constellations on the ceiling at night." Jack glows as he talks about his son.

Rose's lilac room has a flower-and-butterfly theme. Stuffed animals are lined up on a white wicker bed; books are piled on shelves. The kids have a Jack-and-Jill bathroom where both bedrooms have access.

The guest room has a queen-sized, knotty pine bed with matching nightstands, and an *en suite* bathroom. I smell the lavender sitting on a dresser. "You sure know how to welcome a girl."

Jack sets my suitcase beside the closet. "After Sedona, it'll be hard not sleeping together. I think it's best this way until the kids get to know you."

I kiss his cheek. "Good call."

He relaxes and takes my hand. "Come, let me show you the master suite."

Jack's room belongs in Architectural Digest with its pale-peach walls, vaulted ceilings, four-poster king bed, and stone fireplace. Two armchairs frame a window; a vase of dried flowers sits on a round table between them. French doors lead to a balcony with two lounges facing the mountains.

The adjoining bathroom has double sinks, a claw-foot tub, a six-rung towel warmer, and a wide shower. A walk-in closet with customized racks, shelves, and drawers completes the design.

At the tour's end, a strange sensation invades my stomach as if I'm on a roller coaster plunging to earth after a slow, steady climb to the top. Jack's wife may be dead but she is very much alive in this elegant home.

"Charlotte had fun designing this place, didn't she?"

He locks his fingers behind his neck and walks over to the French doors, staring outside. "Yeah, she did."

"Are you sure you're ready for me to be here?"

"Honestly? I didn't think I'd ever bring another woman to this house." He turns and faces me. "Then, I met you."

I rush into his arms, forgetting about first wives and roller coasters. We undress and fall into bed. After making love, Jack holds me as we bask in the late afternoon light. He has made me feel welcome; our reunion couldn't have gone smoother. And yet, I can't stop thinking about Charlotte. She lived here first. Will I ever truly belong in her home?

FIFTY-SIX

J ack nuzzles my neck. "I've imagined holding you like this so many times since Sedona."

"Video chats don't cut it, do they?"

"Not even close."

"How do you manage everything? This house is huge. Who cleans and cooks? Takes care of the kids? Does outside chores?"

"Well, I have a great team. A couple, Sam and Bea, live nearby. Sam oversees the outside, and Bea is my housekeeper and cook. I'd be lost without them. There's Sarah, who watches the kids when I'm not here. My sister Julia helps out. And I couldn't get along without my folks. You can imagine how often we see one another given where we live."

"Will I meet everyone?"

"No. Sarah has the week off, and Sam and Bea are visiting their son in Utah. You'll meet the family, speaking of which"—he glances at a clock—"I better get the kids. They're excited to meet my mystery friend."

"So, that's what I am? A friend?" I tickle his side.

"A good friend. With benefits."

Once we're done laughing, I gather my clothes. "Give me a minute to freshen up."

"You want to come?"

"Of course. Why wouldn't I?"

"Well, the kids are full of energy and the folks are curious. You're safer here."

"I'm tougher than I look."

He taps my nose. "Consider yourself warned."

As Jack pulls up in his parent's driveway, I lower my visor and slide open the mirror. My hair is flat, cheeks flushed. My appearance screams *I just had fabulous sex with your son!* Why didn't I stay at the cabin?

"You look fine." Jack raises his chin at the front porch. "They'll love you as much as me."

Lucas comes barreling toward us. "Daddy's here!"

I flip up the visor. *No turning back now.*

He leaps into Jack's arms. "How's my boy?"

Lucas is an adorable six-year-old with blond hair and light brown eyes. Rose follows close behind, looking as if she might fall at any moment. She's tinier than a typical three-year-old and has dark ringlets, a pale complexion, and an unsteady gait, mostly from wearing ankle orthotics inside her shoes. She's fortunate to get around without a mobility device.

"Me daddy's 'ome!"

She tumbles into Jack's arms. They rub noses, giving each other grins and kisses. "Wanna play game?"

"Not now, honey. Maybe later. There's someone I want you to meet." Jack sets her down; both kids stare up at me.

"Lucas, Rose, this is my friend, Ella. She's visiting us this week, remember?"

Lucas bounces up and down. "I know, daddy. We got her—"

Jack touches his shoulder. "Let's not spoil the surprise, son."

"It's nice to meet you, Lucas." When I extend my hand for a shake, he backs up and holds out his arms, spinning like a helicopter blade.

Rose peeks through Jack's legs. I kneel so we're at eye level. "Hello, Rose. I like games, too. Maybe we can play one later."

Her bashful smile reveals a dimple. She inherited Jack's striking blue eyes and long lashes.

A gray-haired couple stands on the porch. "Well, son, don't keep us waiting. Care to introduce us?"

"Mom, Dad, this is Ella Walker. Ella, meet my parents, Paul and Lillian Thornton."

I offer my hand; Paul brings me in for a hug. "We're happy to have you for a visit, Ella."

"Welcome to Colorado," Lillian says. She turns to Jack. "Do you have dinner plans? I made enough food for everyone."

He glances at me; I nod. "We'd love to stay. Thanks, Mom."

The six of us step inside the house. Flames crackle in the den's stone fireplace. Stacks of newspapers and magazines are piled next to Paul's chair. Toys and books are scattered throughout the room.

I'm in awe watching Jack interact with Lucas and Rose while chatting with his dad. Everyone is at ease, enjoying the moment without ulterior motives. I slip into the kitchen where Lillian is cooking. "May I help?"

"You can set the table if you want." She motions at a hutch. "The plates and silverware are over there."

The beef stew and cornbread are delicious. I love the chaos caused by the kids' outbursts over important things such as not wanting to eat carrots and begging for Lillian's homemade brownies before finishing their meal.

FIFTY-SEVEN

With dishes washed, the four of us say our goodbyes and drive home. The second Jack turns off the engine, Lucas unlocks his seat belt and bolts from the Jeep. "Ruby, where are you?"

Jack opens Rose's door. "Want help getting out, honey?"

"No. Me do it."

He waits patiently as she struggles to unlock her belt, turn around, and slide out on her belly.

Lucas reappears with the dog. "Daddy? Is it time for you-know-what?"

"As soon as we build a fire."

Once flames are dancing in the upstairs fireplace, Jack gives Lucas the green light to retrieve my gift. He races to a closet, removes a wrapped box, and plops it on my lap. "Ta-da!"

"Me 'elp you!" Rose rips off the paper and lifts the lid.

Goosebumps appear when I look inside. The three of them have welcomed me to their world with brown western boots. And not just any boots. These have pink floral patterns on the upper leather with pink-piping edges. They're feminine, unique. Thoughtful.

"Do you like 'em, Ella? Lucas tugs one from the box and hands it over. "Daddy says you live in the city and don't have boots. Everyone wears 'em here."

"Me 'ave 'em, too!" Rose points at her stocking feet.

"They're fantastic! I love the fancy design." I slide them on, tossing a smile at Jack. "How'd you manage a perfect fit?"

"Peeked inside your shoe during Sedona."

I hug each of them. "I have something for you, too. In my room. I'll be right back."

"I'll go with you!" Lucas takes off.

Rose struggles to stand. "Wait for meee!"

I pull the packages from my suitcase, saving Jack's for later. As the kids tear off the paper, I explain the history behind the books.

Lucas mumbles a 'thank you' as he thumbs through the pages.

Rose raises her book. "You read dis now?"

"Honey, it's bath time," Jack says, picking up the trash. "I'm sure Ella will read to you later."

The kids grumble as they follow him to the bathroom. Within minutes, they're in the water with alphabet letters, boats, and other toys. Jack washes Rose as she plays, then dries her off. He lathers her with lotion, dresses her in pajamas, and combs her hair. He repeats the process with Lucas.

Once their teeth are brushed, we settle in front of the fire. Jack reads *The Growing Tree*, and I read Rose's book. The little angel's eyes are almost closed. Jack puts her to bed first, turning on a light that fills the room with stars and sleep music. "G'night, honey."

Lucas resists bedtime; he wants to stay up with us. "We have a lot to show Ella tomorrow, buddy." Jack pats the mattress. "You need a good night's sleep."

Lucas reluctantly climbs in bed and turns on a projector light, transforming his room into the Milky Way. It's quite a spectacle.

"Let's hope he stays put," Jack whispers after closing the door.

I sit on the couch, tucking my feet underneath me. "Do you go through this every night?"

"Welcome to the evening routine." He joins me, yawning and stretching out his legs.

"Are you too tired to open this?" I set a wrapped package on his lap.

Jack studies the package from every angle then looks up at the ceiling, closing his eyes as if in prayer. "Please don't let this be *James and the Giant Peach*. I've read that book so many—"

I poke his ribs for teasing me.

Once we're done laughing, he removes the paper. "Cathedral Rock?"

I nod.

"That was a fun hike." Jack kisses my cheek. "And a thoughtful gift." He puts the frame on the bookcase.

My eyes drift to a photo of him and Charlotte one shelf up. It's not a wedding, family, or other milestone picture. They're on horseback, posed in front of this house during its construction, a reminder of what they built together, of what he lost.

Jack follows my gaze. "Does her photo bother you?"

"No. Not really. Maybe."

"I'll take it down."

"Please don't." Asking him to remove it feels petty. I pat the couch. "Come sit so we can snuggle."

I curl up in his arms. The only sound is the crackling fire, allowing my mind to wander. Meeting the parents went better than expected. And the kids and I seem to get along. Jack is weaving me into his life, step by careful step. It's a journey I never expected, yet it's the only thing I'd wish for if a genie granted me three wishes.

I sneak a glance at the bookcase. It's only a photo. Of two people in love who created babies together. On a higher shelf than our Sedona picture. Jack doesn't seem to mind her watching us. I wish my insecurities agreed.

FIFTY-EIGHT

After breakfast, the four of us put on our boots and go on a walking tour of the ranch. The kids introduce me to their horses, chickens, goats, and pigs. Rose has a cat that hides in the barn and won't come out. Their excited chatter tells me Jack has instilled a love for the land inside of them.

Later, we drive to South St. Vrain Canyon, following a stream that flows through farmland and ranch country. We stop at a park to eat lunch. Jack and I spread a blanket and unpack food while Lucas runs, jumps, and swings, flitting from one activity to another. Rose tries to keep up but tires easily. Instead of getting discouraged, she fills a bucket with sand, twigs, and rocks. Both kids know how to entertain themselves.

Over the next two days, we hike in the Rocky Mountain National Park. We also visit an outdoor market to browse crafts, clothing, food, and pottery. People are friendly—stopping and chatting—more like Italy than California.

On Wednesday, after a slow morning around the house, we drive to Paul and Lillian's home to meet Jack's sister who is helping Lillian cook Thanksgiving dinner.

Julia's eyes brighten as we enter the room. She hops up from the couch, hugging Jack and the kids. She looks similar to her brother—dark hair and blue eyes—but is more animated. Lucas and Rose adore her.

Julia embraces me, whispering in my ear, "Thanks for making my brother smile again."

My cheeks warm, wondering what Jack has told her. I offer to prepare food for Thanksgiving; neither she nor Lillian will budge. They tell me to spend my time with Jack and the kids. The seven of us eat dinner together, then Jack, Lucas, Rose, and I return home.

The kids run upstairs. Jack and I are talking in the kitchen when his phone rings. He looks at the screen, frowning. "Jack Thornton. ... How long ago? ... What'd the MRI show? ... Yes, I understand. I'll be there shortly."

He rubs his neck. "Bad news. A head-on collision resulted in multiple injuries. A colleague is decompressing a spinal cord on one victim. Another has a subdural hematoma. I'm sorry, Ella. I have to go in."

He sighs. "What a day. You've endured my kids' boundless energy, answered more probing questions from my family, and now you get a taste of my work life. I'd understand if you wanted to fly home tomorrow."

I wrap my arms around him. "You're not getting rid of me that easily."

"Good to hear." He pecks my lips and picks up his keys. "I'll take the kids to my folks."

"Or... the three of us can stay put."

He tilts his head. "You sure?"

"Let's ask them."

Jack hollers, "Lucas? Rose? Please come downstairs."

There's a ruckus in the family room; Ruby barks. Soon, feet are clattering down the stairs. He squats in front of the kids. "The hospital called. A lady was hurt in a car accident and needs me to fix her."

"Aww, Dad," Lucas whines. "You said no work this week."

Jack ignores the guilt trip. "Since Ella's here, you can either stay with her or I'll take you to Mimi. Your choice."

Rose wraps her arms around Jack's neck.

Lucas looks at me. "If we stay, can we build the Golden Gate Bridge with Legos?" He's quite a negotiator.

"I'm willing to try."

His smile tells me he's on board. Rose still looks hesitant. "I'd love for you to stay with us, little one."

"You read ca'pilar book?"

"Yes, and you can help with the bridge."

Jack stands, jingling his keys. "So… the decision is Ella?"

Both kids nod.

"All right. Be good for her." He kisses us and hurries out to the garage.

The kids and I stare at one another as the Jeep drives away. Jack is the glue that binds us; his absence creates a void I must fill. I raise my hands, curl my fingers, and tickle their bellies. They laugh loudly enough to cause Ruby to bark. Our happy chaos has returned.

"If you two help me build a fire, I'll make popcorn."

"Yeah!" They scream in unison.

We settle in the family room, munching on our buttered treat and lining up Legos. Rose gets restless and strolls over to the keyboard, playing "Mary Had A Little Lamb" with gusto. Not bad for a three-year-old. Apparently, she inherited Charlotte's musical gene.

"Do you like to dance?" I ask the kids after we finish the bridge.

They stare at me as if I had spoken Mandarin. I suppose dancing isn't on the approved Thornton activity list. We'll have to change that.

I retrieve my phone and press "Viva la Vida" by Coldplay. Soon, the three of us are swirling around the room in rhythm to the music.

They shout, "More, more!" after the song ends.

I play two other tunes, then start their bedtime routine. After reading books, I tuck my bridge-builder in bed first, turning on his night light. "Pleasant dreams, Lucas. We'll see you in the morning."

"Ella? When's daddy coming home? I miss him."

"I'm not sure, honey. Do you need anything before going to sleep? A drink of water?"

"No, thanks." He pulls the covers over his shoulder. "G'night."

When we get to Rose's room, her eyes fill with tears. I hold her on my lap. "What's wrong, little one?"

"Me want dada." Her bottom lip quivers.

Despite consoling her, she remains upset. And who can blame her? Jack is gone, and she's stuck with a near-stranger at night. How can I make her feel safe? An idea comes to mind; I hope it works. Otherwise, I'll call Lillian.

"Want to sleep in my room?"

"Me seep wif you?"

"I miss daddy, too. We'll keep each other company until he comes home."

Rose nods, drying her eyes on her sleeve. She picks up two stuffed toys and off we go. A shower can wait until tomorrow. I change into pajamas and join her in bed. She smells of soap, lotion, and innocence. I'm surprised by how much heat her tiny body generates and how much she wiggles. She hugs her bunny and nestles close to me as we drift off to sleep.

FIFTY-NINE

When I see Rose in bed with me the next morning, I want to take a victory lap. We made it through the night! Those snarled clumps look ominous. Jack brushes her hair after baths but lets her style it during the day, which means it doesn't get combed at all. I wonder if—

Rose's eyes flutter open.

"Hello, little one."

A bashful glow reddens her cheeks; she shrinks away from me.

I pick up her stuffed bunny and alter my voice to sound like a cartoon character. "Hey, Rosie. Wanna dance with me?"

She giggles. "Do dat a'gin."

The door opens. Lucas stands there holding a blanket, a book, and a rocket ship. "What are you two doin'?"

"Acting silly." I pat the bed. "Come join us."

Lucas climbs up with his treasures and settles in.

I latch the bunny to the rocket and fly him around the bed. "Yipee! I'm off to see the moon!"

"Make him go to Jupiter!" Lucas shouts. "And Mars!"

Our astronaut bunny is flying around the universe when Jack leans against the door jamb wearing a wrinkled T-shirt with plaid pajama bottoms. "Got room for one more?"

I chuckle to myself. We're in this huge house, yet the four of us are crammed on my bed.

"Did you have fun last night?" Jack asks the kids.

"You know it!" Lucas shoots to his knees. "Wait until you see our bridge. It's super cool!"

"Me dance wif her!" Rose points at me and shimmies as if music is playing.

Lucas picks up his rocket and puts the rabbit on it. "Catch ya later alligator. I'm flying to San Francisco!" He jumps off the bed and runs into the family room.

"Dat my bunny!" Rose chases after him.

Jack folds me in his arms. "Let them work it out." He nibbles on my neck. "So, last night went well?"

"We had a good time—with one hiccup. Rose missed you and cried so I let her sleep with me. I hope you don't mind."

"Whatever it takes." He presses closer. "Wish I could've seen the dancing."

Sparks ignite that can't go anywhere. "I'd love to give you a private show."

"*Umm*... sound good. Maybe the kids can spend tonight with my folks."

We arrive at the Thornton family home shortly after eleven. Lillian and Julia are in the kitchen preparing a traditional Thanksgiving meal. Lillian wipes her hand on an apron and opens her arms when she sees the kids. "How are my sweetie pies?"

Lucas and Rose rush to her. She finds chores to keep them busy. Julia's husband, Dave, has joined us. He and I take time to get acquainted. Julia takes a break and huddles with Jack for an animated conversation. Paul keeps the fire burning, floating in and out of conversations.

I'm surprised to learn that Jack's thirty-ninth birthday is November 26. The family is celebrating both Thanksgiving and his special day. It's awkward not knowing this milestone ahead of time but I try not to let it bother me. Lillian makes his favorite dessert: apple pie. Lucas and Rose give him framed paintings they made (with the help of their nanny). The adults surprise him with a handcrafted fly-fishing rod, which puts a smile on his face.

The day passes quickly with board games, a walk in the meadow, and eating. Lots of eating. Jack bathes the kids and puts them to bed upstairs, then rejoins the adults around the fireplace. Paul pours several rounds of Amaro, an Italian liqueur made from herbs, spices, flowers, and citrus peels. It has a syrupy, bittersweet taste that goes down easy.

A couple of yawns signal the day's end. Dave and Julia are spending the night, so we're the only ones leaving the house. Jack initiates his departure plan.

"Thanks for the drinks, Dad. Jules and Mom, the food was great. Dave, I enjoyed catching up." Jack looks at Lillian. "I hate waking the kids. Do you mind if I pick them up in the morning?"

"Of course not. We'll see you tomorrow."

Jack and I slip out of the house and hurry to the Jeep. He opens the door for me. "Well? How was your first Thornton Thanksgiving?"

"Day's not over. I owe you a dance, remember?"

He pulls the seatbelt across my chest and clicks it shut, his breath warming my ear. "Oh, I haven't forgotten."

We are barely inside the cabin when our passion explodes. Kissing, touching, groping, mindless lust. We make our way upstairs, tossing clothes along the way, leaving a trail of passion. No thinking, no words, just a carnal drive without inhibition or regret.

Afterward, we lie in each other's arms, satiated. I fall into a dreamless sleep.

SIXTY

I wake to Jack's gaze. "Hi, there." He caresses my cheek.
"Hi, yourself." My face warms as memories return. "Last night got a little insane."

"Years of pent-up desire we unleashed in Sedona. Or the Amaro. I'm not sure."

"You've been gentle, and you've been… Well, like last night. I say we drink more Amaro."

He chuckles. "With you, it's all good." He tucks hair behind my ear. "I love you, Ella. I can't imagine life without you."

My eyes moisten. "I love you, too." The words seem trite—barely conveying the depth of my feelings for him.

"How about spending Christmas and New Years with us? Help us decorate the house? Lyons hosts a parade with fireworks and music in Sandstone Park I think you'll enjoy."

"Count me in." I tap his nose. "I may stay longer if you're lucky."

Jack flashes a wicked smile. "Can that luck begin now?"

The days pass swiftly, and too soon, I must say goodbye to the Thornton family. This time Ruby stays and the kids go to the airport. Jack has welcomed me into the private—and most cherished—part of his life: his family. He and I are on a path to merge our lives. My heart aches as I'm about to fly home.

"Daddy, look! A jet!"

"Yes, son. We're at the airport. You'll see lots of them."

"Why can't Ella stay with us?"

"We talked about this, Lucas. She'll return soon. Let's give her a good send-off." Jack and I share a tender glance.

He parks the Jeep and we walk inside the terminal, riding the escalator down to the security checkpoint. After final hugs and kisses, Jack and the kids retrace their steps as I snake through a long security line.

Three weeks. That's how long until I see them again. I brush away a tear. It feels like an eternity.

I'm walking to the connector train when I hear my name. I look up and see Lucas hanging over the railing, a grin plastered on his face. Jack and Rose are waving. *They waited for me. My family.* More tears arrive as I blow kisses. Christmas can't come fast enough.

SIXTY-ONE

The Piedmont house is too quiet after returning from Colorado. I knew I'd miss Jack but I'm surprised by how much I miss the kids—and our family time.

I settle into a routine but feel tired. I continue to have shortness of breath despite returning to sea level. Even though it's probably nothing, I schedule a same-day appointment with my primary care physician to err on the side of caution.

A nurse records my vital signs and weight before escorting me to a patient room to change into a flimsy paper gown. I read flyers taped to the walls to pass the time, waiting for the door to open.

Dr. Kathryn Lee finally breezes in. "Hello, Ella. How are you?"

"I'm never quite sure how to answer that question while sitting on your exam table."

She smiles and walks over to the sink to wash her hands. "What brings you in?"

"A couple of things. I'm tired even after a full night's sleep. Also, I recently vacationed in Colorado. The altitude did a number on me. I'm still having trouble catching my breath."

Dr. Lee signs onto a computer and reviews my records. "You've lost a few pounds, also. Let's see what's going on." She gloves up and listens to my heart and lungs with her stethoscope then pushes on my abdomen, moving to my neck where she spends extra time. "How long have you had this swollen lymph node?"

"What'd you mean?"

She guides my hand to a tiny, painless bump on the left side.

"I hadn't noticed it."

Dr. Lee finishes the exam and tosses the gloves in the trash. "Let's get some blood work."

"Should I be worried?"

"Not yet." She types on the computer. "If you get your blood drawn today, I'll have the results by tomorrow."

Once she leaves the room, I feel the lump again. It's barely noticeable. I dress, trying not to worry as I make my way to the lab.

My phone rings the next day as I arrive home from a busy shift at the food pantry. "Hello, Doctor Lee."

"Did I catch you at a good time, Ella?"

"You did. Are the lab results back?"

"Yes, and I want to biopsy the lump in your neck."

My breathing halts. "Why?"

"I'm concerned about your white blood count. A biopsy will allow me to make a definitive diagnosis."

Not good. "What are you searching for?"

The line goes silent for a few heart-stopping moments. "I want to rule out lymphoma or other malignancy. Are you able to come in next Tuesday at ten-fifteen?"

My hand flies to my mouth to suppress a gasp. "I'll be there."

Lymphoma? Malignancy? This can't be happening. Not again. Not to me. Not now. Fresh air. I need fresh air. I change into walking shoes and head out the front door.

My neighbor waves from a window. Doesn't Susan have anything better to do than to monitor my every move? I up the pace.

Crap. Yes, I mean crap. I stepped in squishy dog poop. It's practically steaming on the sidewalk. Can't owners pick up after their pets? What's wrong with people? I scrape the stinky mess on the curb and keep moving.

Dr. Lee sounded worried. What if the biopsy is positive? What if there isn't a—

Two boys kicking a soccer ball back and forth in Crocker Park break my train of thought. A man and woman are sitting on a bench, sipping coffee and watching them.

This family makes me think of Jack and the kids. He would never obsess over the lump or jump to conclusions. Instead, he'd have the biopsy, wait for the results, and act accordingly. He'd maintain his routine and not speculate. I'd be wise to do the same. Should I tell him and Tara what's going on? No, I don't think so. Why worry them unnecessarily?

SIXTY-TWO

On Saturday, Tara and I meet for breakfast at Yali's café in Berkeley. We load up on avocado toast with poached eggs. Once she gets her caffeine fix and I finish my smoothie, we drive to Tilden Regional Park.

The chilly day has chased away the crowds. As we hike the Seaview Trail to the top, Tara distracts me from my worries by describing a *pro bono* case she recently handled. A social worker asked her to intervene after a dad broke his son's arm by heaving him against a wall. Tara got a restraining order for the mom and found a room for them at a shelter. How could a father do that to his son?

I lighten up the conversation with stories about Jack and the kids. She laughs when I tell her about my cowgirl boots. "Those summer camps at Rawhide Ranch are about to pay off! Yee-haw!"

I double over in laughter. Friendship is the best medicine.

Jack and I text multiple times each day and occasionally talk on the phone. Saturday is our date night when we video chat after the kids are asleep. I search for my confident voice this evening.

"I miss that handsome face."

"That's exactly what this tired dad needed to hear."

"Tell me about the kids."

"Lucas got a library book about the Golden Gate Bridge. He added string to your bridge and is excited to show you. Rose wanders into the guest room searching for you. She doesn't quite get the concept of time. We're ticking off days on a calendar until you return."

I do my best to stay upbeat during our conversation. Afterward, I walk outside and look into the ebony sky. There's not a star to be seen.

"Hello up there. Are You listening? I can't imagine You leading me to Jack and his children and not letting me take care of them. That's not how You work, right? I'd appreciate a sign letting me know everything will turn out fine. How about a spotlight moving across the sky? … A gust of wind? … What about a siren? Ambulance or police; it doesn't matter.

No response. Nothing but gut-wrenching silence.

Three days after the biopsy, Dr. Lee's assistant calls and asks me to come in for an appointment. A four-alarm fire bell sounds in my head. It's bad news. Otherwise, I'd receive an email link to my portal page, see the word NEGATIVE next to pathology, and get on with my life.

I drive to the medical building, trying not to panic. A nurse does the vital signs routine, then drops me off at Dr. Lee's office.

"Hello, Ella. Take a seat." She picks up a folder on her bookcase, then drops it on the floor, papers flying in all directions. "Sorry about that." She gathers them and swings around, bumping her elbow on the desk. "Not my day."

Dr. Lee is always calm and in control. Nothing rattles her. A cold sensation seeps throughout my body. She's about to blow up my world.

"I know you're eager to hear the results so let's get to it." She hands me a lab report. "The biopsy showed Reed-Sternberg cells, which are indicative of Hodgkin's disease, also known as Hodgkin's lymphoma."

"Hodgkin's?"

"It's a cancer of the lymphatic system that's caused by a mutation in your white blood cells."

I sit there shell-shocked, unable to talk.

"I've ordered a chest x-ray and CT scan to determine the lymphoma's stage. The results will allow us to customize a treatment plan for you."

Dr. Lee softens her voice. "Ella, I imagine this news is difficult to hear, especially given your family history. Remember, this cancer is highly curable. You can live a full life."

Her attempt to console me fails miserably. I have to get out of here before I suffocate.

SIXTY-THREE

I flee the medical office and drive straight to the Marin Headlands, tears blinding my vision. The last time I came here, baby Sophia had died. Now, my life hangs in the balance.

The day is cold and dreary. Fog nearly shrouds the entire bridge; only a glimpse of its orange arch appears. Tears fall fast and furious. Hodgkin's lymphoma. Cancer. Again. People stare and I don't care. William Walker is right. I am damaged goods. What did I ever do to deserve this fate?

Jack, Lucas, Rose, and I were on our way to becoming a family. This diagnosis has turned me into a thousand-pound anchor that will drag them to the ocean's floor. I'll bring misery to their lives instead of joy, tears rather than laughter. No matter what Dr. Lee says, she and I both know the truth: I'm a cancer magnet. I got lucky once and beat the disease. The odds are stacked against me this time.

I stagger along a wooden fence, the wind making a low-pitched wail as it whips chilly air against my face. Insects buzz in the tall grass;

car tires crunch over loose gravel. I keep walking until I'm alone. So alone, so broken, so unworthy.

The ocean's turbulent water creates foamy whitecaps down the coast. Jagged rocks form craggy paths up and down the shoreline. A gull soars in front of me, gliding on thermals and updrafts, floating and dipping, free of worry and disappointment. I climb over the fence. Rocks dislodge, tumbling into the water.

"Will you teach me to fly, little bird? Let me join you? Show me an easy way out?" I hold out my arms, ready to close my eyes.

"Ma'am? Are you all right?"

A park ranger stares at me from several feet away.

"The wind's picking up," he cautions. "Might be safer on this side of the fence."

More gulls sail past, flapping wings, swooping and squawking, beckoning me to join the colony. The choppy sea crashes into giant tombstone rocks hundreds of feet below. A flash of lightning brightens the sky, followed by a crack of thunder, a few drops of rain. One jump and it's over. No more cancer or pain.

"I care about you, ma'am. May we talk?"

Air or land? Which way do I step?

"Ma'am, don't do this. You are a young woman with a whole lot of future in front of you. Please. Take my hand. Let me help you."

I turn toward the panicky voice. Instead of a stranger's sweaty face, I see Tara and Jack, Lucas and Rose. I see my mom, dad, grandfather. Neighbors and friends. I see the faces of babies I've nursed back to health and hundreds more who need me. I see reasons to accept the man's outstretched hand.

The ranger helps me over the fence.

"I dropped an earring and was looking for it."

His eyes drift to my ears. "Looks as if you found it."

I touch the small hoops, both snugly in place. I hug the civil servant, walk to my car, and drive home.

SIXTY-FOUR

On Friday, December 9, I arrive at the hospital to have a chest x-ray and CT scan. Dr. Lee is searching for enlarged lymph nodes and lesions. Once I learn where I stand, I'll decide what to tell Jack and Tara.

This week's date night with Jack worries me. Texting is easy because I control my words and emotions. Video chatting is different. Last week I fooled him. I don't think I'm capable of another award-winning performance. I'm worried he'll see through the charade.

I take my neighbor's dog on a walk ahead of time. Having Ollie trot alongside me, sniffing or peeing on every tree, telephone pole, and fire hydrant is a welcome distraction. I return home to await Jack's call. Surprisingly, I hold up my end of the conversation but it's not easy.

That night I wake up around 3:00 a.m. with soaked pajamas. I log onto the Internet and learn night sweats are a symptom of Hodgkin's, another symbolic nail in my coffin. I send Dr. Lee a message, then turn on the TV to binge-watch the first season of Breaking Bad. Poor Walter White has more troubles than me.

Today is December 13, the day I learn my fate. Is the cancer contained or has it spread? Is my condition curable? I drive to the medical office, praying for a holiday miracle.

Normally, I love watching the town evolve into a living fairytale. This year's red, green, and gold transformation seem garish. The music on the radio sounds maudlin. Watching a skinny Santa smoke a cigarette in front of the Salvation Army's iconic red kettle is wrong on so many levels.

People with coughs, sneezes, and runny noses gather in Dr. Lee's waiting room. I, on the other hand, appear perfectly normal. They are probably thinking: *Why is she taking up space?* Hypochondriac. Now, that's a word to embrace.

A nurse leads me to Dr. Lee's office, bypassing the exam room. I cling to a photo of Jack and the kids for strength.

"Hello, Ella." Dr. Lee waits for me to sit. "Are you ready to hear the plan?"

Right to business.

She opens a folder. "The x-ray showed lymphoma in only one lymph node. This is good news. We found the disease early. Unfortunately, the CT revealed a suspicious shadow in your left lung." Dr. Lee breaks eye contact, shifting in her chair. "Because of your weight loss and night sweats, we must assume the disease is more advanced and requires aggressive treatment."

There will be no miracle for me.

Dr. Lee pushes over a tissue box. "I spoke with an oncologist. He's recommending a combination of chemotherapy and radiation to treat the disease."

"It'll be intense, won't it?"

"Yes, and what's waiting for you at the end is a likely cure. Are you ready to fight?"

I don't want to fight anything. I want to go home, curl up, and pretend this isn't happening. I fought ovarian cancer and ended up with a hysterectomy. I know how this fighting business works. Someone gets hurt. Me.

"When will the chemo start?"

"In January. It's done at the Infusion Center as an outpatient. You'll recover at home."

"What poison will you use?"

Dr. Lee flinches at my word choice. "The oncologist recommends a four-drug combo: Adriamycin, Bleomycin, Vinblastin, and Dacarbazine. Each works in a different way to kill the cancer cells."

And everything else in their path. "How many cycles?"

"Eight. Following chemo, you'll have five weeks of daily radiation for the lymphoma in your neck."

I close my eyes, absorbing the plan. It feels as if I'm standing at home base holding a bat as five MLB pitchers heave fastballs at me. How will my body survive the assault?

"So, my dance card is filled through next June?"

Dr. Lee nods, offering a supportive smile.

"Any promise of a full recovery?"

The smile fades. "We'll do everything within our power to make it happen, Ella."

No money-back guarantee for me.

I return to the bleak world with little hope. My cancer has already spread. Treatment is aggressive and uncertain. Ho, ho, ho. No Merry Christmas for me. Or Happy New Year. Or Valentine's Day. Or Easter. A cancer plan replaces Jack's plan to blend our lives.

My eyes roll heavenward. "Thanks for teaching me what getting stabbed in the heart feels like. I had no idea You were so cruel."

SIXTY-FIVE

I t's time to tell Tara about the Hodgkin's. She agrees to come for dinner on Friday night. I hand her a blended margarita as she arrives. She takes a long pull, smacking her lips. "Delicious!"

I turn on the gas fireplace. "Have a seat. I made your favorite appetizer."

She tells me about her father's birthday party while scooping guacamole with salty tortilla chips. When she diverts the conversation to me, I focus on our meal. I have no intention of ruining her appetite with my news.

After eating, we bring our drinks to the living room. Tara pats her stomach. "That was one terrific meal." She settles into a chair. "Catch me up with Jack and the kids. You haven't said much about them."

I finish my margarita. "Will you be my mainstay?"

"What?"

"I have Hodgkin's Lymphoma, a type of cancer. I'm about to undergo an intensive combo of chemotherapy and radiation. I want you as my support person."

Tara looks at me as if I'm playing an April fool's joke on her. I pass over a copy of my treatment plan.

She studies the paperwork, her eyes filling with tears. "Oh. My. God. How is this even possible?" She rubs her forehead. "What does Jack say about the diagnosis?"

"He doesn't know and never will."

"What's that supposed to mean?"

"I'm ending the relationship."

"You're *what*?"

"The last thing Jack needs is another problem to drag him down."

She jumps to her feet. "Are you kidding me? You have to tell him, Ella. Let him decide whether or not you're a *problem.*"

"Last July, his family sent him to Italy because he was depressed."

"So? How does that relate to you?"

"Don't you see? I'm one more burden! It's better this way."

"For who? Jack? Or you?"

"The decision is made. It's not fair dragging him into this mess when he lives in Colorado. I don't want him feeling guilty because he can't be here."

"You are—"

"Stop!" I hold up my hand. "This isn't about Jack! It's about us! Will you help me or not?"

Tara freezes, looking as if she got caught sneaking into her parent's house after curfew. I run over and hug her. "I'm sorry! I didn't mean to yell."

We sit together on the sofa, taking a minute to compose ourselves. Once things cool down, Tara says, "What does a support person do?"

"I'd like you to meet my doctor, come to key appointments. I'd also appreciate you staying the first night after chemo. I got pretty sick last time."

"Done." Tara enters Dr. Lee's information in her contacts and adds my appointments to her calendar. She opens a browser and types. Her face brightens. "According to Stanford, Hodgkin's can be cured if found and treated early. That's you, Ella! You'll likely have a full recovery!"

I get up and stand in front of the fireplace. "First, I have to get through the next six months."

"It'd be easier with Jack's support. Tell him, Ella. Give him a choice. Don't make the biggest mistake of your life by not trusting him."

As she talks, the tears return. "If—and this is a big if—I recover, I may reach out to him. But I won't drag him or his children into this ordeal now. I want you to drop it."

Tara closes her eyes and sighs. She takes our glasses to the kitchen and washes them, then puts on her coat to leave. She presses her hands on my shoulders. "You *will* beat this monster, Ella. It doesn't feel like it now but you will be cured. And I'll be at your side every step of the way."

I walk her outside, watching her taillights get smaller. I can't let her opinions about Jack sway me. She has no idea how much he has suffered. Forcing him to worry about a sick girlfriend who lives twelve hundred miles away is not an option.

On Saturday evening, I wait for Jack's call. He's later than unusual, probably got roped into reading an extra story. When my phone rings, I don't answer. I call him on the landline to avoid seeing his face.

"Why didn't you answer the video?"

First lie. "I have four percent on my phone."

"It isn't from texting me. I've missed hearing from you this week. What's going on?"

Follow the script. "I've made a decision, Jack. I'm not coming to Colorado over the holidays." *Two more lies.* "The altitude bothers me and I don't like snow." *The sad truth.* "I have commitments in California. I apologize for springing this news on you at the last minute."

The line goes silent.

"Jack?"

"I heard what you said but don't understand. We had a plan. You're supposed to be here in three days." His voice sounds down-hearted, dejected.

"Plans change. We lead such different lives. Since I'm not moving to Colorado and you're never coming to California, I don't see a future for us."

"Didn't seem that way when you were here at Thanksgiving. Or in Sedona."

It's so hard to lie to him. If I don't hang up soon, he'll pull the truth out of me. "My life is here, Jack. Please respect my wishes. Don't contact me again." *Click.*

He calls right back.

One ring, two rings, three, four, five. Voicemail. "Ella! Don't do this. Talk to me!"

I cover my ears to block his voice as I crumble to the floor, tears raining down my cheeks. If I told him about the Hodgkin's, he'd feel obliged to help; it's how he is wired. I won't do that to him and the kids. I'm not dragging them into my miserable, cesspool life.

SIXTY-SIX

After two days of not returning Jack's calls, the phone stops ringing. Never in my life have I felt such sorrow.

I remain home the entire holiday season to avoid germs since treatment will be postponed if I get sick. No Christmas tree, no parties. No outings with Tara. No more working at the food bank. Everything meaningful in my life has been stolen by an invisible, greedy enemy intent on destroying me.

Did Jack decorate for the holidays? I bet he dragged a twelve-foot Douglas fir upstairs to the family room. The tree wouldn't be perfect like those in malls. Instead, its lights and popcorn garlands would be woven through branches in uneven strands. I can picture tinsel tossed randomly, ornaments dangling on lower limbs, put there by tiny, excited hands. The top would either have a glowing star or an angel holding a candle. The tree would be the prettiest one I had ever seen.

On January 4, Tara drives me to the Cancer Infusion Center to begin the fight for my life. I sit on a cushioned chair in the communal treatment room, looking through windows at manicured shrubs, raked gravel, and a man-made waterfall. Very Zen.

My medical team gets busy. A doctor educates me about the drugs and their potential side effects. I sign the consent without reading it. I already know the treatment is voluntary, that I'm free to withdraw at any time. No one has to spell out the associated risks and adverse reactions that will decimate my body, nor do they need to highlight that I might die from the treatment, which is supposed to save me. If anyone actually read these forms, hospitals would be empty.

A social worker hands me literature about support groups, which I have no intention of attending. I won't sit in a circle with other cancer patients, rehashing our sad stories. It's too dismal.

A nurse pricks my skin and inserts a needle in a vein, hitting the sweet spot on the first try. Within minutes, the four-drug combo is flowing through my body like a well-trained army marching to war. Each heartbeat pushes the poison toward a target: cancer cells, healthy cells, major organs. Shoot! Kill! Destroy! Take no prisoners! The battle has begun.

Nausea arrives almost immediately. Medication does little to stop the horrible sensations invading my body. On the way home, Tara drives carefully but it doesn't matter. Every stop and go, each turn results in me filling a vomit bag.

Once home, I crawl in bed, hoping the lack of movement will calm me. It doesn't. When I close my eyes, the earth spins, sending me to the porcelain god where I pray for my misery to end.

Diarrhea arrives seven hours later and weakens me even more. The symptoms fade two days later, and I slowly rebuild my strength. There are moments when I want to return to the Headlands and fly with that bird.

It's in these darkest hours that Jack and his children sustain me. I hold their photos close to my heart. They take me to a better place, tricking my mind into believing there's hope.

Ten days after the treatment, I drive to the lab for mid-cycle testing. Since the chemo attacks both healthy and cancer cells, my doctor must confirm I'm strong enough for another round of poison.

Tara brings me food and quits asking how I feel. Instead, she asks what I need. She checks on me as her schedule allows; the days march forward.

It's been three weeks since the first chemo treatment, and I'm at the Infusion Center for round two. I put in earbuds and listen to Enya's "Shepherd Moons" album as the drugs enter my body. Minutes later, the nausea beast visits. Not even Enya has the power to save me.

Tara arrives at one o'clock to take me home. She's fidgety, jingling her keys. "I'm sorry, Ella, but something came up. Urgent business. I'm taking you home and getting you settled, then leaving for a couple of hours. It's unavoidable."

I pinch my lips so I don't lash out. She knows how sick I get on chemo day. Why not get someone else to handle the crisis?

Riding in the car triggers nausea again but this time I try a different technique. Instead of fighting the assault, I surrender, letting the misery pass through me. It doesn't work. Up comes the poison and down goes my hope.

The second chemo round delivers two unwanted gifts: the beginning of hair loss and mouth sores. Tara mixes water, baking soda, and salt to swish around in my mouth. Although the concoction tastes awful, it soothes the discomfort. I wish there was a cure for drug-induced baldness.

Tara looks at her watch. "I need to go. My mom will come over if you want company."

I'm tempted to take her up on the offer but don't want to burden anyone else, especially Tara's mom. She's busy with the family's bakery.

"I'll be fine. Just please hurry back."

SIXTY-SEVEN

Shortly after Tara drives away, I run to the toilet and retch until nothing is left except dry heaves. I clean up the mess and crawl into bed. Being alone when you're this sick is terrifying.

I'm curled up feeling like yesterday's garbage when I hear the front door open. Thank God, Tara's back. She walks straight to my bedroom. "You still alive?"

"Barely. I want to take a bath and—"

Two sapphire eyes stop me mid-sentence. "Hello, Ella." Jack sets a travel bag on the floor.

"What … why …"

"I'm here to take care of you. Do you want to take a bath?"

Nausea hits at the wrong moment. I race to the bathroom. Tara pulls my hair away from my face as I vomit. "For the record," she whispers in my ear, "I didn't call him; he called me. He's a keeper, Ella. Please listen to what he has to say."

Once I'm back in bed, Jack walks Tara to the front door. I hear their voices but can't make out the words. He returns to my room and stands at the foot of the bed. I guess he's waiting for me to make the first move.

"What'd Tara tell you?"

"Everything."

I'm embarrassed by how I look and smell. I don't want him seeing me this way. "Who's with the kids?"

"My folks. Why didn't you tell me about the Hodgkin's?"

"Because you're here instead of with Lucas and Rose."

Jack kicks off his shoes, climbs in bed, and holds me. "You're not going through this alone, Ella. Let me know when you're ready for a bath."

I melt into his arms. He's paused his regular life to come here. Why pretend I'm not happy to see him? "Tara told me I should've confided in you."

"Tara is a wise woman."

By mid-afternoon on the second day, I'm well enough to sit in the family room without running to the bathroom every fifteen minutes. Jack has been a wonderful partner, making sure I have what I need. Right now, he's standing in front of a window, watching water droplets streak the glass. Is he thinking about the kids? His work? Does he regret coming to California? What's his endgame?

"I appreciate you taking care of me, Jack. I'm sorry to be such a burden."

"You're not a burden, Ella. Why would you say that?" He turns on the gas fireplace.

"Because treatment lasts through June with no guarantee of a cure. I'd say that qualifies me as a burden."

"I'm sure your doctors mentioned the ninety percent cure rate for localized lymphomas. The Hodgkin's is a bump in the road."

"It's more of a giant sinkhole where people get swallowed up."

He sits next to me on the sofa. "You can't lose hope, Ella. Two kiddos in Colorado miss you very much."

"What will you tell Lucas and Rose when the chemo fails?"

"First, we'll probably never have that conversation since the odds are in your favor. And second, I'm raising my kids to prepare them for life—not protect them from it. They know things don't always go according to plan."

"You need to protect them from *me*. This is the second time I've had cancer, Jack. My body is broken."

He tips his head back, blowing air through his lips. "Okay, look. Do I wish you weren't sick? That we didn't have to deal with this setback? Of course. But that's not our reality."

He leans forward, resting his chin on folded hands. "When Tara told me about your health, I sat on the news for a week. I've had many sleepless nights over your situation, Ella. I didn't fly here on a whim."

"Why did you come?"

"To ask you to move to Colorado."

My stomach knots up. This is exactly why I didn't tell him about the Hodgkin's. He wants to turn my life upside down when I need stability.

"I can't leave California."

"What's holding you here?"

"For starters, I'm in the middle of treatment with a team I trust."

"One of my friends is a renowned oncologist. He has agreed to take over your care. I'll make sure the transition goes smoothly."

I wave my hand across the room. "What about this house? I can't just up and move."

"Why not? You have an alarm, a gardener. Your neighbor—that woman and her dog—will keep an eye on the place until you decide what to do with it. The post office will forward mail; there's electronic banking."

I cross the room to escape his pressure tactics. "Do you realize we've only spent twenty-one days together, including Will's hospitalization? Twenty-one days, Jack. That's no time at all for this type of commitment."

The only sound in the room is the rain's pitter-patter against the windows. Jack picks up a decorative pill and spins it. "Here's a question for you. When you flew home after Thanksgiving, before you knew about the lymphoma, how'd you envision our relationship progressing? Be honest."

I pick at imaginary lint on my robe. "I would've spent several weeks over the holidays. Then, I'd find a reason to return. Again and again."

"Until you stayed forever?" He tips his head, smiling. "Did we arrive at the same conclusion?"

"Visits and long-term plans are off the table until I'm in remission. It's not up for discussion, Jack. You and the kids have been through enough trauma."

He twirls the pillow again then sets it down. "Ella, I know I'm asking a lot. I also know if I was the sick one, you'd do anything to help me." He joins me in front of the fireplace, pulling a paper from his pocket. "Please, let me help you."

He passes over a flight itinerary. Both of us are scheduled to fly from Oakland to Denver in three days. He's already bought my one-way ticket. I wad up the paper and toss it into the flames. "You're not listening to me, Jack."

He presses a hand on the mantel, watching the red embers curl the paper and turn it into ash. "The thought of moving to another state must feel daunting. You're comfortable in this home. You trust your doctors. You have Tara nearby. I can't imagine how scary getting cancer twice must feel. And I understand why you want to shield me and the kids after what happened to Charlotte. I have heard you, Ella."

He faces me, weaving his fingers through mine. "I still want you to come home with me. I believe not only will you be cured but we will turn twenty-one days into forever. But I won't pressure you anymore. If you decide to stay, we'll figure out the best way for me to support you long distance."

I stand there with a lump in my throat, tears filling my eyes. It's remarkable how the right words said at the right time and in the right manner can shift one's thinking. Jack didn't come to California out of pity or obligation or guilt. He's not here to rescue me or to convince me to do something I don't want to do. Jack is here because loves me. All of me. Even the broken parts.

This man has taken a huge leap of faith and is asking me to do the same. I hug him with all of my strength and hold on tight. Our lives are about to change in unimaginable ways.

The next few days are a whirlwind of activity as we pack and ready the house for my departure. We visit the medical office for lab work and to see Dr. Lee for the last time.

Jack shakes her hand. "Thanks for diagnosing Ella quickly and for starting her on a path to recovery."

"I spoke with Doctor Stevenson yesterday and sent him Ella's file. He's ready to take over her care." Dr. Lee hands me a prescription. "I recommend you take this for motion sickness. You may want to reserve a wheelchair at the airport so you don't exhaust yourself walking through the terminal."

"I appreciate everything you've done for me, Dr. Lee."

"You're in capable hands, Ella. Please stay in touch."

Tara stops by the following morning to say goodbye. After she leaves, Jack and I lock up the house, give my neighbor a key, and take a shuttle to the airport. As we drive away, a heaviness lingers in my chest. Despite Jack's heartfelt words, moving to Colorado feels rushed, uncertain. I hope we don't regret using my illness to force this bold move.

SIXTY-EIGHT

The flight to Colorado is difficult to endure—even with Jack by my side. The constant movement makes me nauseous the entire trip. Medication doesn't help whatsoever. Sitting upright in a cramped space for hours has decimated me.

I wait on a bench as Jack retrieves the Jeep. Once we're on the highway, I lie back and take in the scenery. I've missed Colorado's crisp mountain air. The clouds float in the clear sky, bending and parting to the rhythm of a slow song. A recent storm has painted the mountain peaks white.

The house is lovelier than I remember. Jack's housekeeper and cook, Bea, is waiting for us. She's an efficient-looking, approachable woman in her mid-fifties.

"Welcome home, Jack. And you must be Ella."

"It's nice to meet you, Bea. I'm looking forward to—"

My knees buckle; Jack catches me. "You're exhausted. Let's get you to bed." He picks up my suitcases and we climb the stairs. As I turn toward the guest room, he shakes his head. "Not there. My room."

"What about Lucas and Rose?"

"They know you're living here now. I want you with me."

His manner convinces me he has thought through this decision. I shower, put on pajamas, and crawl under the covers, wanting to sleep for two days. Bea enters the room carrying a tray.

Jack has her put it on my nightstand. "Chemo causes dehydration, which saps energy and sinks moods. Vomiting pulls nutrients from your body. Bea and I partnered to develop a plan to address these issues."

"Jack told me about your cancer, dear. I boiled sliced ginger for this tea, a time-tested remedy for nausea." She lifts a thermos. "This vegetable broth was made from scratch. It'll warm you and provide nutrition. The blueberries and crackers will digest easily."

Jack raises his chin at the door. "I'm picking up the kids. Do you need anything before I go?"

I squeeze his hand. "I'm fine."

He kisses my cheek and walks out with Bea.

Winter sunlight pours into the room, warming my face. I dreamed of a future with Jack, although this is nothing as I imagined. I think about that night in Italy when we saw those locks on the fence, the ones where couples threw away the key to seal their love.

Jack put our lock on the fence when he came to California. He threw away the key when he brought me here. My eyes fill with tears over my vulnerability and his generosity. I hope all of this works out.

SIXTY-NINE

The grinding sound of a garage door wakes me from a nap. I sit up and hand-brush my hair, listening to small feet on the stairs. I've dreaded this moment since leaving California.

Jack cracks open the bedroom door. When he sees me awake, he opens it all the way. The distrust on the kids' faces crushes me. Not only did I break my promise to visit them over the holidays, but I also stole their dad for a week. On top of that, they're stuck living with my illness, changing the household's dynamic. How will I ever make this up to them?

I open my arms wide, inviting them over. "I'm so happy to see you both!"

Lucas gives me a cursory hug. He's nothing like the rambunctious boy I met at Thanksgiving. Rose won't budge from Jack's arms.

"You look different," Lucas says matter-of-factly. "Daddy says you're sick. What's wrong?"

No beating around the bush with this little man. "What'd daddy tell you?"

"That you have a bad bug in your body and you'll get better with medicine. He said we have to help. Want me to read to you?"

"I would love that, Lucas."

He bolts from the room, allowing me to focus on Rose. I play peekaboo, trying to engage her. She buries her face in Jack's neck. No smile for me.

Lucas returns with two books; one is *The Growing Tree*. "I can read the story by myself. That's one cool tree!" He slides in bed and thumbs to the first page. "Once there was a giving tree who loved a little boy. And every day the boy—"

"Wait for meee!" Rose scrambles from Jack's arms and settles in beside her brother.

Lucas starts reading again, and once we're immersed in the book, Jack slips away, leaving us alone. Two books, a heartfelt apology, and a few tickles return some trust between us.

By the third day, I'm feeling more like myself. During Thanksgiving, Jack built a schedule around me. Now, I get to watch their regular lives unfold.

The alarm rings at six-thirty every weekday morning. Jack showers and dresses then gets the kids ready for school. It's downstairs by seven-forty where Bea has breakfast waiting and lunches packed. At eight sharp, Jack drives Lucas to school and then goes to work.

Sarah, the nanny, takes Rose to a private preschool at nine. Sarah is a gifted artist who paints while the kids are in school. She brings them home in the afternoon where they play outside, weather permitting. Otherwise, they do various inside activities.

Bea cleans the house, grocery shops, does the laundry, and cooks. She fusses over Jack and the kids as if they are family. Jack arrives home around six. Sarah and Bea debrief with him, then leave for the night.

At six-thirty, the four of us eat the dinner Bea prepared. We load the dishwasher, then go upstairs for the evening. There's no television in the Thornton home, nor does Jack allow the kids to have iPads. They talk, paint, build with Legos, read, make music, or play board games. Bath time is at seven forty-five followed by storytelling with lights out by eight-thirty.

Jack's only quiet time is when the kids are asleep. He's drained yet his day doesn't end. He takes care of home business and mentally prepares for his next workday, especially if he has a complex surgery.

Tonight, he and I are snuggling on the sofa in front of a cozy fire after tucking the kids in bed. The photo of him and Charlotte on horseback is gone from the bookcase. I scan other shelves to see if I missed it. Their wedding photo as well as several with her and Lucas are still there but not the horseback one.

"I took it down," Jack says, reading my mind. "I'm not erasing Charlotte from this house but it's your home now. We'll display our pictures."

Words escape me. I can't do much for him right now but think of a small thing. "Will you please lay your head on my lap?"

He gives me a curious stare as I move to the far end of the sofa, allowing him to stretch out. "Close your eyes."

I use my fingertips to massage his scalp in slow, circular motions until his breathing slows, his shoulders relax, and his worry lines disappear. He nuzzles his face against my belly.

This gifted surgeon and devoted family man leads a non-stop, pressure-filled life. He craves a soft place to land and has chosen me as his landing spot. That's why he sacrificed so much to come to California. Jack needs me as much as I need him.

I catch my reflection in the bay window. That Higher Power who keeps playing chess with my life is lurking out there in the darkness. I hope he's listening to my thoughts.

I was furious at You the last time we spoke. I'm still upset over the Hodgkin's but it is what it is. Can You and I start over? I'll do anything You ask, finish every treatment. I'll not miss a single appointment. Just don't take me away from Jack and these innocent children, not after bringing me here, not after inserting me into their daily lives. Do we have a deal?

I wait for an answer, a signal that He has heard my plea. There is no shooting star or flashing light. No tingling sensation. A crackling fire and my partner's gentle snores are the only sounds in the room. For now, that's enough.

SEVENTY

We're eating breakfast when the phone rings, and from what I can tell, the nanny is calling in sick.

Jack looks at me, rubbing his chin.

"I'd love to step in," I tell him.

He smiles and turns to Rose. "Honey, Sarah isn't coming today. Ella will take care of you instead."

"Me go to 'chool?" Her eyes ping-pong from Jack to me.

I kneel so she and I are at eye level. "Yes, and I'll take you. It'll be our special day."

"You picking me up?" Lucas drags a piece of waffle through syrup.

"Of course. Maybe I can meet your teacher."

"That'd be cool."

Jack jots down addresses and gives me the key to an older Jeep he owns. It comes equipped with booster seats (and a toy basket), allowing Sarah and others to safely transport the kids.

Lucas and Jack take off while Rose and I finish breakfast. Hair hangs in her face. She's wearing blue-striped pants with a yellow polka dot blouse and purple socks. She often looks like this and no one seems to notice. Today I'm in charge. I'm not letting her go to school looking like a ragamuffin.

"I love your pants," I tell her. "Does it come with a matching top?"

"Me like dis one."

Strike one.

"What if I run upstairs and get white socks for you?"

Rose looks at her feet, scrunching her nose. "Me got socks."

Let's try this from another angle. I retrieve a brush and two barrettes from the downstairs bathroom. "Want me to put these pretty clips in your hair?"

She takes the brush and skims her hair, making it even frizzier. "Aw dun."

So much for my influence.

She holds up a shoe. "You help wif dis?"

It's not what I had in mind but it's a start.

Cerebral palsy is a motor disability that affects a person's ability to move and maintain balance and posture. Rose's traumatic delivery most likely damaged her brain, leading to this condition. Orthotics support her weak ankles, correct her pronated feet, and help with hip rotation. She's six months delayed in language skills and has marked weakness in her legs, arms, and hands. I'm curious how her private school addresses these disabilities.

Rather than dropping her off and leaving, I get permission from the school's director to stay and observe. An occupational therapist asks Rose to remove her shoes, then sits with her at a table and has her mold shapes with a resistive, hand-strengthening material called TheraPutty. Next, she has Rose dress a doll in various outfits. The zippers, buttons, and ties give her hands a robust workout.

"Lydia is waiting for you," the therapist announces forty-five minutes later. "Let's see how fast you can put on your shoes."

Rose asks for help like she did this morning. Instead of intervening, the therapist encourages her. "Keep going! You're almost there!" When Rose finishes, she raises both arms and shouts, "Me did it!"

I shake my head. The little stinker duped me at the house. She knows she's supposed to put on her shoes. The exercise strengthens her hands. I vow never to make that mistake again.

Next comes physical therapy. The therapist, Lydia, lays out a ladder-like course on the floor. She asks Rose to put one foot in a square, lift her other leg, and step into the next square. Rose falls a few times but keeps going until she passes through twelve squares. Lydia holds Rose's hand in a different exercise as she steps sideways on a wide beam, picking up stuffed toys from the floor. Rose acts as if they're playing a game when, in fact, the whole routine is part of a core-strengthening exercise. I'm getting valuable tips on how to incorporate therapy into home activities.

Even the lunch routine has a purpose. A teacher passes out plates with food to students who are sitting at a semi-circular table. A speech pathologist sits in front, asking each child to name the plate's color and describe its contents. An impressive amount of language work is done during mealtime. No wonder my little rebel exudes independence. This entire program nurtures it. Today has been a real eye-opener.

Rose naps at school and has afternoon activities such as music and art, which extends her day to three o'clock. When I attempt to leave at twelve-thirty, she cries. I try calming her without success. She wants to come home with me and I don't know how to say no. It's my fault for breaking her routine. I choke down guilt and bring her to the cabin, playing until it's time to retrieve Lucas from school.

Spending the day with Rose triggered questions about her health. That evening, I sit with Jack in the family room after putting the kids to bed. "Are Rose's seizures under control?"

"She hasn't had one since September. The phenobarbital and phenytoin combo seems to be working." He sits back, crossing his legs.

"Rose said you stayed at her school and brought her home early. How come?"

My stomach knots up over the abrupt change in topics. Is he upset with me for changing her routine? Disappointed in my judgment? What if–

I halt my runaway thoughts. I'm talking to Jack, not Will. He isn't attacking me. We're having an adult, two-way conversation. *Be yourself.*

"I wanted to see how the school manages her disabilities."

"What'd you learn?"

"You found an exceptional program for her. The occupational, physical, and speech therapies are well-coordinated. Lots of work is done in a short time. I also discovered ways to help her."

"Such as?"

"It's important to speak in shorter sentences. Something like *'Rose, it's time to take your bath'* becomes *'Bath time.'* Also, I need to let her do things for herself. For example, putting on her shoes strengthens her hands. And I know why you bought a trampoline. The jumping strengthens her legs and core."

"All true." He tilts his head. "Why'd you ask about her seizures?"

"I'm used to caring for preemies, not a three-year-old with CP. I want to feel confident handling the situation if she seizes when we're alone... like this afternoon, which, by the way, won't happen again. I mean I expect to be alone with her, just not when she's supposed to, you know, attend school."

Jack chortles. "May you have more success saying no to her than me." He goes on to explain seizure management, then pretends to faint.

His silliness cracks me up. "What are you doing?"

"I better give you a CPR refresher, too. You never know when you'll need that valuable skill."

Before I can respond, he drags me on top of him. We make out like two teenagers in the backseat of a car at midnight.

Oh, how I love this man.

SEVENTY-ONE

The weeks ebb and flow around my health and family. The cancer center is close to Jack's office, and he drives me on chemo days. When he can't, the Thornton family rallies around me.

Bea's cooking and home remedies help me recover faster. During the day, I explore the ranch. The meadow has become my sanctuary with its trees, flowers, birds, deer, and other wildlife coming and going.

Bea's husband, Sam, has introduced me to my riding horse, a tall, big-boned Friesian with a dark coat and a thick mane named Coco. I'm guessing she used to belong to Charlotte although no one mentions ownership. Coco has a calm demeanor, which is what matters to me.

Talking with Tara keeps me grounded. I sent her a photo of my bald head; she mailed a floral scarf telling me to wear it so I don't scare the kids. I texted her a photo of me wearing the gift, holding a chicken. She texted back: *Who are you and what did you do with my best friend?*

It's the end of March, and my mood has grown as gloomy as the land-scape. Even though Jack goes out of his way to include me, I struggle to find my footing in this busy household. Most days I feel like an actor making a cameo in our home movie.

Jack says I have a seasonal slump. He assures me it's temporary. Right now, I'm riding a stationary bike that he set up in our bedroom by a window. Sunlight and exercise are supposed to improve my mood. How is that possible when the weather forecast is cloudy with a chance of despair? And pumping pedals to nowhere gives me too much time to think.

About Sarah, for instance. She is a wonderful nanny but I want her job. Let me take care of the kids. Bring her in when I'm sick. Why can't Jack put me in charge of transporting Lucas and Rose to and from school and helping with homework? I'm able to take them to the dentist. Why relegate me to the sidelines?

And then there's Bea. Whenever I offer to make dinner, she nudges me out of the kitchen saying Jack pays her to cook. Don't get me wrong. Bea is a talented chef and we're lucky to have her, but I enjoy cooking, too.

Pump, pump, pump…

I transferred my nursing license to Colorado, hoping to find a job. Most openings require working nights and/or weekends when my family is home, something I won't do. Jack and the kids are my top priority. I did find a part-time job as a Discharge Planner that had perfect daytime hours. The telephone interview was going well until I mentioned my cancer. Suddenly, the recruiter was looking for someone with more experience. So much for the Americans with Disability Act.

I pedal harder, hoping to leave my pity party in the dust. After all, I have books to read, trails to hike, a terrific medical team, and evenings and weekends with my family. Plus, I get to take care of the kids when Jack is called away.

"Ella?" Bea shouts from downstairs. "I'm going grocery shopping. Do you need anything from the store?"

I hop off the bike and traipse downstairs. "Want company?"

She taps a finger on her chin, glancing outside. "It's about to snow. I'd feel better if you stayed inside and kept warm. We don't want you getting sick."

My hope for an outing disappears down the gravel road as Bea drives to town without me. I wish she didn't treat me like a porcelain doll. I glance at the kitchen. Two brown-speckled bananas trigger an idea. I'm making Lucas and Rose's afternoon snack!

I search for a healthy banana bread recipe and find one that swaps oil for applesauce. Perfect. I get to work measuring flour and sugar, whipping in eggs, vanilla, and other ingredients in a bowl. I have a purpose!

When the oven is ready, I slide in the baking dish and set the timer. I scrape the mixing bowl with my finger, enjoying every luscious lick. The kids will love this recipe. I'm washing dishes when the doorbell rings. A UPS driver and I exchange waves before he climbs into his brown truck and speeds away.

I finish cleaning up, then pad over to the front door to see what he left behind. It's a package from my attorney. Inside are two files. The first one is a financial statement, resurfacing my unease about not contributing to Jack's budget. He flat-out refuses to take any money.

The second file gives me my freedom: final divorce papers from William Charles Walker. Emotionally, our marriage ended months ago; this document makes it official. He and I never talk or text. He has no idea I've moved to Colorado or that I have cancer. I'm sure he and Jenna are busy getting ready for the baby. Are they having a son? Daughter? Will they marry now that he is free? I hope he'll be a good dad.

It's snowing outside; flakes float to the ground in silent wonder, creating a layer of shimmering, silver ribbons on the earth. A deer nibbles vegetation in the meadow. Usually, the graceful animals arrive in clusters. This one is foraging alone. Like me. Damaged goods. A tear slips down my cheek.

Bea treats me like a porcelain doll because I am fragile. How else do you explain a thirty-year-old woman getting cancer twice? Jack knows this, too. It's why he keeps Sarah around.

SEVENTY-TWO

Today is Saturday, May 12, Lucas's seventh birthday. Luckily for me, chemo is over and radiation hasn't begun, putting me in a feel-good zone.

The four of us pile into the Jeep and drive to The Wonder of Science at Twenty Ninth Street in Boulder to explore an interactive exhibit. Lucas is super excited to see the large-scale lighted planets and a thirty-five-foot-sounding rocket used in atmospheric studies.

The birthday boy's eyes widen as we step inside the building. He runs to the rocket first, then flits from one exhibit to another. Rose can't keep up so we divide and conquer. Jack sticks with Lucas; I move at Rose's pace.

Afterward, we drive to the Pearl Street Mall, a four-block outdoor pedestrian area. Lucas chooses a pizza lunch at Nick-N-Willy's and gets a "Happy Birthday" serenade by everyone in the restaurant. He blows out all seven candles on his chocolate cake.

Lucas spots a kite shop on our way to the car and drags Jack inside. He talks his dad into buying a dragon for him and a purple butterfly for his sister. Who can deny the birthday boy anything?

It's a quiet ride home as Rose plays with an Etch A Sketch and Lucas reads kite instructions. We're cruising along when Lucas says, "Ella? Are you my mom now?"

The out-of-the-blue question catches me off guard, leaving me tongue-tied. I'm unsure how to respond.

"What makes you ask that question, son?" Jack smiles at me.

"I want a mom and Ella's a nice lady."

"Yeah, she is." Jack glances in the rearview mirror. "Ella loves you, Lucas. She enjoys looking after you. Since that's what moms do, I suppose that makes her yours."

"Cool. Can I call her 'Mom?'"

"If that's what you want."

Rose chimes in. "She my momma, too?"

"Yes, honey. Yours, too."

I choke back tears. This moment should be joyful, a moment to celebrate. Jack has recognized me as his children's mother, a dream come true. Instead, the exchange exposes my darkest fear: What if the treatment fails?

Jack clasps my hand. "Don't worry. Everything will turn out fine."

I wish I had as much faith in my cure as him.

SEVENTY-THREE

Lucas wants to fly his kite as soon as we get home so the four of us hike to an open space between the house and barn. Jack explains the basics, and before long, the dragon is up in the air, looking menacing with its sharp teeth and long tail.

Rose doesn't have the same luck with her butterfly. No matter how hard she tries, she can't get it airborne. Naturally, she refuses our help. She missed a nap and is tired. I take her inside for a snack to avoid a complete meltdown.

She is coloring in the living room and I'm cutting an apple in the kitchen when a strange noise causes me to look up. Oh, no! My girl is on the floor, her body arched, eyes rolling backward. Her muscles spasm, jerking rapidly.

I drop the knife and run to her, pulling the coffee table out of the way and turning her sideways to prevent choking. I yank a crayon from her hand, watching helplessly as her body works through the seizure. I yell for Jack but he's too far away to hear me.

Although the episode lasts less than a minute, it's the longest minute of my life. After the shaking stops, Rose is dazed yet unharmed. I pull her limp body onto my lap.

"You're okay, sweetie. I'm here." I rock back and forth, comforting her.

The boys come inside, kicking off their boots. Jack spots us on the floor and rushes over. "What's going on?"

"A full-blown seizure."

"Oh, Rose. You were doing so well, honey." Jack tries taking her but she clings to me. "Want momma."

I hold her securely. "Daddy and I are here. We won't let anything happen to you."

Jack sits back, rubbing his forehead. "We need to get blood work to learn what's happening with her meds." He gestures at her wet pants. "Will you change her while I calm Lucas? We'll meet in the Jeep."

Two and a half hours later, we return home from the hospital exhausted. We put the kids to bed and collapse on the sofa.

"I'm worried about leaving her alone, Jack. What if she seizes again?"

He yawns, stretching out his legs on the ottoman. "Her meds were increased. She'll be fine."

"But…"

"I understand your worry." He rests his hand on my thigh. "I've been around this block a few times. We'll check on her later. For now, she needs to sleep."

This entire day has been devoted to kids. I might as well keep the momentum going. "May I show you something?"

"About Rose?"

"She's part of it. I'll be right back."

I return, holding the packet from Mr. Abrams. "My lawyer sent these files to me. It'll explain where I stand financially. I also have an idea to run past you." I hand him the quarterly report. "Please read the summary page."

Jack does as asked, taking his time. He returns the file, looking amused. "So, not only are you a loving partner and a terrific mom, you come with money. What more can I ask?"

"Jack, this is serious. I want to find a way to contribute to our household. Please hear me out."

He nods, linking his fingers behind his head.

"This report doesn't include my house. Colorado is my home now. It's time to sell the California property."

"Makes sense to me."

"There are two things I want to do with the proceeds. First, I want to donate half to Tara's law firm. Starting a nonprofit has been her dream. She's done so much for me this past year. Giving her the seed money to set up a foundation is my way of thanking her. I think my mom would approve of using the money this way."

I take an extra breath. "I want to use the remaining cash to establish trust funds for Lucas and Rose."

Jack tenses. "Ella, that isn't necessary."

"Hear me out. Rose has disabilities. They both have hefty education expenses coming up. This money will help them become their best selves. It's how I want to contribute financially to our family."

He leans forward, tapping his lips with folded hands. "You've put a lot of thought into this generous offer. Let me mull it over."

I'm tempted to plead on the kid's behalf but don't. Jack likes to ponder issues before making decisions. At least he's considering the proposal.

"I'm glad you think of Colorado as home," Jack says. "When's your divorce final?"

"The papers arrived two months ago."

"Well then, let's get married, make our relationship official. It's time for a new last name."

Not where I expected this conversation to go. I untie my headscarf and dangle it, the fuzz on my scalp a stark reminder of our precarious future. "I want to wait until treatment is over before making that commitment."

He tugs the scarf from my hand, weaving it through his fingers. "The outcome won't change how I feel, Ella. I want you as my wife."

His heartfelt words bring tears to my eyes. I'm ready to throw caution to the wind and run to city hall when Jack ties the scarf around his head and makes a goofy face. "Don't you want me as your husband?"

I playfully punch his arm. "You had to ruin the moment, didn't you?"

We both have a good laugh.

"Just know," he says with a straight face. "I'm ready to take that next leap whenever you are."

SEVENTY-FOUR

After Rose's seizure, Jack installs a camera in her room, which transmits her image to a monitor in the master suite, giving me peace of mind. Sarah gets a paid vacation while I keep a close eye on my girl.

For one week, I experience full-time motherhood. There are squabbles, tears, and tantrums, as well as love, laughter, and amazement. I embrace every minute. I remember thinking of the babies at my former hospital as surrogate children. The real deal is a thousand times better.

May 17 begins the final phase of my cancer treatment: Involved Field Radiation. This therapy targets the lymphoma on the left side of my neck. A CT scan pinpoints the radiation zone, and I get my first tattoo: an ink dot to mark the spot.

For five weeks, I have this treatment Monday through Friday. The procedure takes thirty minutes to set up and one to deliver. The radiation is pain-free, and the side effects are slight fatigue and minor skin irritation. Compared to chemo, this therapy is a breeze instead of a hurricane. The treatment does take me away from the kids, relegating me to the sidelines once again. I remain positive, not missing a single appointment. I'm keeping my eye on the prize.

June 21 is an important milestone. Not only is today my last radiation appointment, but after six grueling months, it's also the end of my entire treatment plan. I have fought the battles; I did everything asked of me. Now, I must wait several weeks to undergo testing, which will reveal the winner of the cancer war.

As I leave the radiation center, I think about the past year. Fate brought two fractured souls together in Italy and didn't stop intervening until a new family was formed in Colorado. One of those happily-ever-after stories, right? Not necessarily.

I met a forty-year-old college professor named Molly at a support group. Three years ago, she was diagnosed with breast cancer. Even though she did everything asked of her, cancer has spread to her brain, leaving her husband and two daughters devastated.

Is it my destiny to marry Jack? To raise a family? Do I get to attend soccer games and piano recitals? Watch Lucas and Rose grow into thriving adults? Revive my career? Or will my time on earth be counted in months like Molly? Will I follow her down a path of hospice and sorrow?

I chase away the doomsday thoughts and focus on happier ones. My girl is turning four next week; I have a party to plan.

As I drive to the store to buy birthday supplies, my mind drifts to Tara. Thanks to her, my California house is in escrow. I can't wait to see her expression when I give her the seed money to start a nonprofit. As for the rest of the cash, Jack has agreed to let me set up smaller trusts for Lucas and Rose, insisting I keep some money for me. No matter my fate, I have peace of mind knowing my children will have a quality education. I pray I'll see them receive their diplomas.

SEVENTY-FIVE

Today is Friday, July 27, the most important day of my life. Seventy-two hours earlier, I completed a full diagnostic workup. I'm a bundle of nerves as I drive to the oncologist's office. Will I be cancer-free? If so, I have a family to raise. If not, where do I go from here?

Dr. Stevenson is Jack's colleague and friend. He has been a strong advocate during my treatment. He glances up from his computer when I arrive at his office. "Morning, Ella. How are you?"

I sit across from him. "I believe it's you who will answer that question today, Travis. How am I?"

He smiles. "Is Jack joining us?"

"No. He's working." My leg bounces so fast I worry it'll launch me into outer space. "The results?"

He opens his computer and reads a document aloud.

I hold my breath. "Does this mean what I think it means?"

"The treatment worked, Ella. You're in remission."

I gasp, covering my mouth. "I'm cancer-free?"

"Your lungs are clear, and no cancer cells were detected in your lymph nodes."

I sit there shell-shocked, having a hard time believing his words after everything I've gone through.

"It's not every day I get to deliver such positive news." He breaks eye contact briefly. "Lymphomas do have a sneaky way of recurring. I'll need to monitor you with lab tests and CT scans. For now, I'm giving you a clean bill of health."

I hug him, unable to contain my joy. "Please don't say anything to Jack. I want to tell him."

"He'll want to see these." Travis prints out the test results and passes them over. "Wish I could see his face when you deliver the news."

Rather than driving straight home, I stop at a park to let my new reality settle in. As I stroll along a path, the trees and flowers seem extra colorful, the sky bluer, the birds sing louder.

I am whole again. The cancer is gone. No more sideline observer or porcelain doll or cameo roles for me. No more drowning in constant fear. I won the war. I get to raise my family, dust off my resume. I get to live!

A man tosses a ball for his dog to chase as two boys play tag. Children are climbing on a jungle gym as two women sit and talk, keeping an eye on their little ones. A gopher pops his head through a dirt mound, checking out the action. I glance at my cowgirl boots and smile, knowing I'm part of this close-knit community.

Last summer in Italy, I thought of myself as a poorly assembled jigsaw puzzle. Linking the right pieces took courage, fortitude, and faith. I circle back to the car, excited to slide the last piece into place.

SEVENTY-SIX

It's Friday evening, and Jack will be tired from a busy week. As the garage door opens, I light candles. It's often chaotic at this hour because of the kids. Not tonight. This evening, a quiet home, a table set for two, and a big announcement awaits him.

"Hi there." He kicks off his shoes. "Where are the kids?"

"Mom and Dad wanted them to spend the night. I hope you don't mind."

"So, it's only you and me?"

I nod, hanging up his jacket. "You hungry?"

"For you." He nibbles my neck and works his way to my lips.

I'm tempted to let him keep going but I have other plans for us. "Bea left early so I cooked. I made your favorite dinner."

"I get grilled trout *and* an evening alone with you?"

"Me and the trout, yes. Grilled, no. I'm trying a new recipe. I simmered the fish in olive oil, garlic, capers, butter, lemon, and fresh parsley."

He licks his lips. "Bea should leave early more often."

We have a relaxing meal, talking about what's important to us. Later, we sit outside on the porch to let the food digest. Tonight's sunset brings fiery red and apricot hues cascading across the sky.

Jack drapes an arm around me. "Nice way to begin the weekend."

At the right moment, I sit up. "I'm in the mood for a bubble bath. How about you?"

"And the evening keeps getting better." He stands, pulling me up with him. "I always enjoy a good soak with you"—he winks—"and what comes after."

We climb the stairs, fill the tub, and light candles. Jack settles into the bubbly haven; I follow, nestling against his chest, my favorite place to be.

Ten minutes later, I pick up the lavender soap. "May I wash you?"

"Mm-hm." He closes his eyes.

I take my time massaging his shoulders, chest, and arms. Tension drains from his body; he's relaxed without a care in the world. I have him where I want him.

"I love you, Jack Thornton. I love you more than the room in my heart."

His eyes drift open.

"I want to take care of you, Lucas, and Rose for the rest of my life. Will you marry me?"

"What's going on, Ella?"

"I'm ready for that final leap."

He sits up, water sloshing around us. "You had the tests?"

"I'm cancer-free, Jack. I'll show you the reports later. Will you marry me?"

He cups my face, his eyes pooling with tears.

"Well?" I press. "Do I get your last name?"

"You already know the answer."

We dry off and move to our bed. Jack holds me in his arms. "Why didn't you tell me about the appointment, Ella? You knew I wanted to be there."

His somber tone breaks my heart. My decision to exclude him has hurt his feelings, something I never intended.

"I wanted to spare you pain in case the news was bad."

He rolls up on an elbow. "Life isn't only about the good times. Promise me you'll confide in me. No secrets. Let's do this together."

I nod like a bobblehead doll. "Can we fire Sarah? I want her job." The shroud has lifted. I want to embrace motherhood in every way.

He chuckles. "I'm surprised you waited this long to ask."

SEVENTY-SEVEN

Jack and I wake the next day excited about our future. We decide to marry on the ranch in a simple ceremony. He studies every page of my test results. "These are very promising, Ella. Let's go tell the folks."

Lucas and Rose are on the front porch when we arrive. We hurry from the car and scoop them up.

"I milked the cow!" Lucas says proudly.

"Me feed da chikins!"

Jack and I smother them with kisses.

"Lucas? Rose?" Lillian says. "I left blueberry muffins on the table for you." She holds the front door open. "We'll be in shortly."

Once the kids are out of earshot, Paul says, "What's going on with you two?"

Jack tells them about my test results. Lillian pulls a tissue from her pocket and pats her eyes. "My prayers have been answered."

"We want to marry soon," Jack says. "Not too big. Something on the ranch. Family and close friends. Are you two up for some planning?"

"Nothing would give us greater joy," Lillian says.

After a short visit with Paul and Lillian, we return home. Jack directs the kids to the kitchen table. "Take a seat, please. Mom and I have some things to tell you."

"But I want to fly my kite!"

"In a minute. Family meeting first."

Lucas grudgingly slides into his spot; Rose follows.

"Sarah is leaving us."

"Why, daddy?" Lucas tilts his head like his father. "Who'll pick us up from school?"

Jack raises his chin at me. "Your mom."

Both kids look at me. "Remember when I first came to live with you? How I was sick? Well, the doctors made me better. Now, I have more time to spend with you."

"And that's not all," Jack says. "We're having a party in a few weeks."

"Yipee!" Lucas claps his hands. "Who's having a birthday?"

"No birthday." Jack rubs his chin. "It's a family party. Mom and I will talk to each other. Your job is to dress in fancy clothes and have fun. Sound good?"

"Okey dokey, daddy pokie." Lucas bounces, making the bench squeak. "Now, can we go outside?"

Jack shakes his head. "Yes, son. Want to join us, Rose?"

"No. Me stay wif momma." She tugs my hand. "Wanna play domnos?"

I kiss her cheek. "You betcha."

Jack and I look at each other and shrug. We thought the kids would have more questions. Instead, it's just a regular day at the cabin.

Later that evening, I email my test results to Dr. Lee. I also call Tara to tell her about the remission. Her loud squeal makes my ears ring.

"That's the *best* news ever! It's time to celebrate!"

"Funny you should mention celebrating. Want to be my maid of honor for the last time?"

"You know it! When's the big day?"

"We're considering August 25th or September 1st. Can you get away?"

"September isn't good. Let's see what's going on in August." Tara pauses. "Yeah, that works."

"Yay! You book a flight and I'll get your dress. We're having a slumber party!"

SEVENTY-EIGHT

It's Friday, August 24th, and I'm driving to the Denver airport to meet Tara. I circle until I spot her waiting curbside. I park, jump from the car, and rush to her. "It's so good to see you!"

"You look amazing!" Tara tugs on my short hair. "It's growing out nicely." She glances inside the car. "Where are Jack and the kids?"

"At the cabin. I wanted time alone with you."

"Works for me."

We hop in the car, picking up where we left off six months earlier, volleying conversations, never running out of topics. When we get to Boulder, I pull into a parking space at Chautauqua Park.

"Why are we stopping?"

"So we can talk without interruptions. That won't happen with the kids around."

Tara nudges my arm. "Careful what you wish for!"

I ignore her teasing while strolling down the Royal Arch Trail.

"This place is gorgeous, Ella."

I point at reddish-brown sandstone rock slabs. "Those are the Flatirons, home to some great hikes."

Tara lifts her foot, wiggling a Vans slip-on. "Not exactly hiking quality."

"We'll go another time. Today, we're sticking to this path." I loop my arm through hers. "Thanks for selling the house."

"Your neighbor's real estate friend did the heavy lifting. My family had fun rummaging through the place after the movers took your stuff. Dylan thanks you again for his graduation gift."

"I'm glad he likes the car."

Tara grins. "He asked about the ring in the ashtray."

"Ring?"

"I'm guessing it's your wedding ring from the evil one."

"Yeah, I took it off when we flew to Italy. Tell your brother to sell it for gas money."

"With pleasure."

Tara looks as if she wants to gossip about Will but I'm not interested. I distract her by pointing to a pine grove. "Let's go hang out over there."

Once we find two comfortable rocks to sit on, I remove an envelope from my purse and hand it to her.

"What's this?"

"A gift for you. Open it, please."

"You're the bride. Shouldn't I be giving the presents?"

"Open it!"

"Okay, okay." Tara slips her finger under the seal and removes a check made out to her law firm for seven-hundred-thousand dollars. "What's this?"

"I remember you saying you'd do more *pro bono* work if you had the funding. I want your dreams to come true. Here's the seed money to start a nonprofit foundation."

Tara's jaw drops. "No way, Ella. I can't accept this."

"It's already done." I try not to cry but tears flow anyway. "You're the best friend a girl could have, Tara Marie Collins. You took care of me when I was sick. You guided me through a living hell with Will. Now, I'm marrying the love of my life and get to raise two incredible kids. This money is nothing compared to the miracles you made happen for me."

By now, Tara is crying, too. "Spend it on your family, Ella. Not me."

"If you don't take it, I'll get upset. And you don't want to agitate a cancer patient. We're fragile."

Tara leans her shoulder into me. "I thought they cured you."

"Tell me you don't want to help more people like that boy who broke his arm when his dad threw him against a wall. If you say no, I'll keep the money."

"Wow. You know how to throw a punch." Tara stares at the check. "Okay, I gratefully accept your gift. I won't disappoint you."

"You never do." I stand and pull Tara up with me. "Let's go home. Jack and the kids are waiting for us. You'll love his barbeque ribs."

SEVENTY-NINE

August 25th is a glorious morning as I wake on my wedding day. Jack spent last night at his parent's house so he wouldn't see me until the ceremony. Lucas went with him, giving me a chance to introduce Rose to her first slumber party.

My girl liked playing host yesterday, taking Tara on a tour of the ranch. Watching the power attorney and four-year-old jump together on the trampoline made my day.

Tara sealed their friendship by showing Rose how to use an iPad. Rose's face lit up when the three of us climbed into Tara's bed with popcorn to watch *Beauty and the Beast* on the small screen late into the evening.

I fear I opened Pandora's Box by letting Tara demonstrate the device's tempting features. Jack hasn't allowed this technology (or television, video games, etc.) in the house, wanting the kids to develop their brains without dependence on screens. I understand his reasoning, and I also see a place for electronics in moderation. But that's a conversation for another day. I toss back the covers. It's almost ten o'clock, time to shake a leg.

I rouse my girls out of bed with promises of pancakes, bacon, and smoothies. After breakfast, we listen to music as we get ready for the wedding.

Rose has never had her nails painted; she loves the shiny polish. She looks adorable in her cornflower blue dress. A flower wreath holds her ringlets in place. Jack and I set her orthotics and sturdy shoes aside for this one day, replacing them with glitter ballet flats. She calls them her party shoes.

Even though Tara's powdered blue satin dress is too frilly for her taste, she's a good sport about wearing it. I weave her curly red hair into a flattering up-do with wispy tendrils framing her face. When Rose tells her she looks like Princess Belle, Tara pulls out her phone and scrolls to a photo of her in a power suit standing in front of her law building. "This is what real princesses look like."

Rose scrunches her nose, looking at me for answers. I think they both make valid points, merging imagination with reality. I encourage them to keep talking while I slip away to finish dressing.

My white, full-length column gown is simple but elegant. I love its one-inch shoulder straps and draped cowl neckline. I feel beautiful, not from the dress but from knowing I'm about to become Jack's wife. I hope he likes the gown, though.

The eighty-four-degree day has transitioned into a pleasant evening, the sun sending orangish streaks across the sky. Lavender lupine and yellow prairie sage dot the fields leading to the Rockies. The ceremony will be held in our meadow inside a wooden gazebo that Jack had built for my thirty-first birthday. Thanks to Julia, my sanctuary is filled with colorful, fragrant flowers.

Jack and Lucas are mingling with guests. My groom is handsome in a black suit, white shirt, and blue tie. Lucas's brown pants and cream vest make him look older. Both had their hair trimmed.

To begin the festivities, a harpist plays my mother's favorite Bach composition: "Cantata No. 147, Jesu, Joy of Man's Desiring." The music brings her spirit to the wedding. Jack takes his place in the gazebo with his dad, the best man. Lillian and Lucas sit together in the front row.

As the harpist switches to Pachelbel's "Canon in D Major," Tara and Rose stroll in time with the music, dropping red petals along the way. Tara settles Rose with Julia, then stands upfront with Jack, exchanging smiles and a few words.

Anticipation builds as the harpist strums Mendelssohn's "Wedding March." I glance into the sky hoping to catch a glimpse of that elusive Higher Power to thank Him for this day. He and I have traveled across oceans, met in caves and faraway villages. We have survived dark hours and had inspirational moments. He is nowhere to be found, yet I see Him everywhere: the clouds, the mountains, the flowers. Every sunrise and sunset. I find him in my children's laughter, Tara's friendship, and especially in the man who is waiting for me at the end of this flower-strewn path.

"Welcome, Jack and Ella," the minister says as the music fades. "Family and friends have gathered today to share in your joy. The journey to this moment has not been easy, yet here you stand, more resilient than ever to commit your lives to each other. In a world filled with uncertainties, you have shown us that faith, love, and courage conquer all."

The minister faces the audience. "Jack and Ella have written vows for this blessed occasion." He steps back. "Please begin when you're ready."

Jack and I face each other, linking our fingers. Instead of talking right away, he looks at me in a way that voices commitment better than any words. That ever-present connection between us hums like electricity.

"Ever since I watched you help that boy in Italy, I knew you were a special woman. You are fearless yet kind, always giving of yourself to others. Lucas, Rose, and I are fortunate to have you in our lives. I eagerly anticipate the chance to grow as a family and to fall in love with you more each day. I promise to cherish you no matter what life brings. You have my love, my trust, and my fidelity for the rest of our days." He presses his forehead against mine. "And you look gorgeous in that dress."

I take a moment to compose myself before reciting my vows. "You are a man of integrity, Jack Thornton. I see your values play out every day with your children, with me, and in your work. You live an authentic life and have more compassion than anyone I have ever met. I am so grateful you found a place in your heart and home for me. I promise to walk by your side and to always be your soft place to land. Thank you for trusting me with Lucas and Rose. Let's make Charlotte proud by how we raise them. Lastly, and this is important so listen up. I commit to being your devoted photo assistant for as long as we both shall live."

Jack chuckles. "Glad that pick-up line worked."

Laughter ripples through the audience.

"I'm not sure about that last comment," the minister says, "but everyone can see the affection you two have for each other. It's time to exchange rings."

Jack's father hands him my platinum band. "Today, I place this ring on your finger, a symbol of the unbroken bond between us. May it remind you of the love we share, today and always."

Warmth flows through me as he slides the ring into place. There is no doubt or hesitation. We are strong individually, and better as a team. Tara passes over Jack's matching band.

"This ring is an unbroken circle that embodies my love for you and the kids. May it always remind you how much I cherish our life on this ranch. I'm so excited to become your wife, Jack. I can't wait to see what we accomplish together." I slide the ring on his finger.

The minister steps forward. "You have witnessed Jack and Ella's commitment to each other. It is my honor to declare they are husband and wife. Jack, you may kiss your bride."

Our first kiss as a married couple sends me over the moon. The moment is sacred, binding, transcendent.

The minister has us face our guests. "Ladies and gentlemen, I'm pleased to present Doctor and Mrs. Jack Thornton."

Just as the audience claps, Lucas jumps to his feet. "Hey! What about me and Rose? You said this was a family party!"

Everyone turns and stares.

Jack and I smile at each other. "Yes, son, we did." He whispers to the minister, then motions for the kids to join us. He holds Lucas; I pick up Rose.

The minister chortles. "Shall we try this again? Ladies and gentlemen, I am thrilled to present the Thornton *family*."

My precious son is beaming when he shouts, "Let the party begin!"

I couldn't agree more.

AUTHOR'S NOTE

Thank you for reading the second edition of my debut novel, *The Vernazza Effect*. I hope you enjoyed traveling with Ella on her remarkable journey to find her destiny.

Reviews are crucial for authors, and even just a line or two makes a difference. Please consider posting one on Amazon, Goodreads, and/or your favorite review site to help other readers discover this story. Your word-of-mouth referrals are greatly appreciated.

In 2007, I spent three glorious days in Vernazza, which inspired this novel. Visiting the Cinque Terre left an indelible mark on my life. I encourage you to visit this special place on earth so its magic rubs off on you, too.

Best wishes, Roberta

ACKNOWLEDGMENTS

My husband is my biggest fan and supporter. Not many spouses would beta read a romance novel twice. Andy always improves my work.

Debbi Kightlinger is my Tara Collins. She converted me from a tourist to a traveler, and she inspires me with her passion. I'll never forget our getaway to Italy.

My editor, Carol Callahan, has taught me so much about the writing process. Her voice is always in my head, whispering advice as I create and edit.

Deb Strand painted the Vernazza watercolor that became the book's cover. The painting brings me such joy every time I look at it.

My two wonderful daughters, Kimberly and Kristy, keep me grounded with their encouragement, love, and humor. Their ability to successfully juggle career and family never ceases to amaze me.

Thanks to my little ones, Camden, Collette, and Sierra, for helping me breathe life into Lucas and Rose just by being their sweet selves.

Cheryl McCaughan's friendship and encouragement mean the world to me. She gave me my first "how-to" book on writing fiction.

My cousin, Gloria, is a gifted writer. Our conversations about the writer's life always inspire me.

I treasured the day Janet Mills drove me around Piedmont's neighborhoods, parks, and cemeteries for research.

Gratitude goes to The Magnolia Park Early Start Program (Cathy, Frances, Linda, Lori, Wendy,) and CCS (Lydia, Monika, Susan). The work they do is inspiring.

ABOUT THE AUTHOR

After a rewarding career in health care, Roberta R. Carr became a full-time writer. She enjoys creating slice-of-life stories to entertain you as well as to stir new thoughts. Her travel experiences usually weave their way into the plots.

She has published five novels: *The Vernazza Effect*, *The Foundation*, *The Bennett Women*, *The Things We Don't Say*, and *Clara's Way*. She co-wrote the non-fiction book, *The 8th Field Hospital*, with her husband about his experience as a physician in the Vietnam War. She also co-wrote the children's book *Vanessa's Rotten Day* with her granddaughter, Collette.

Roberta lives in Novato, California. She is always working on a project but makes time for her family and friends, a morning walk, chai, and travel. To learn more about her work, please visit www.robertacarr.com. You can also follow her on Facebook to receive writing updates.

THE SAGA CONTINUES

In *The Vernazza Effect*, you met Ella's best friend, Tara Collins. To learn more about Tara and what she does with that $700,000 gift, check out my novel, *The Foundation*, a haunting tale about sex trafficking. Available on <u>Amazon</u>.

www.ingramcontent.com/pod-product-compliance
Lightning Source LLC
Chambersburg PA
CBHW022152170626
46807CB00005B/2177